Shine Through the Gloom

Mike,

May 2021 be an
excellent year of
celebrations for you.

Best Mark.

Shine Through the Gloom

Mark Crabtree

SUNESIS MINISTRIES LTD

Shine Through the Gloom

ISBN 978-0-9956837-3-0

Published by Sunesis Ministries Ltd. For more information about Sunesis Ministries Ltd, please visit:

www.stuartpattico.com

Contents

I dedicate this book to the jewel in my crown. A truly amazing woman.

Characters

Nigel Hawkson	-	Owner of Club
Mike Phillips	-	Current Head coach
Tony Jeffs	-	The Motivator
Billy "Big Mac" McGrath	-	Tactician extraordinaire
Clay Jackson	-	A jewel in the crown
Charles Hayworth	-	Dj to "HP" radio
Sam Ryan	-	Rough diamond geezer
Graham Krusher	-	The Secret Weapon
Mark Dellany Smith	-	The running man
Darren Phillips	-	Troubled son of Mike
Frank Malone	-	The Volcano
Kieran Samson	-	Homeless man
John Vossa	-	The ageing warrior
Giovanni Corbisiero	-	Life long fan of HPR

1

A faded memory resurfaces

Of course, there was no mention from Tony about the aches and pains he was suffering from after last night's Power League exertions. He'd used the time well; not only to hang out with his 16 year old son, which of course he enjoyed, but also to help restore his boy's confidence and faith in the game of football.

You see, after Nate's two hip operations, a couple of seasons sidelined, and a lot of moaning and groaning from the coach and his fellow team mates, Tony decided Nate needed a timeout. And he was right; Nate was struggling. Exams were just round the corner, his soon-to-be ex-girlfriend was taking a lot of her troubles out on him and his teammates were giving him grief because he couldn't run like he used to.

A local church team played in a Monday night League and were looking for temporary players, so Tony managed to convince his boy to go along. The game was played with a high tempo and was surprisingly competitive. Initially, Tony was slightly concerned as one of the regular players had a habit of whining at his teammates for not aspiring to the standard of play he expected, but to be honest, the chap needed to take a good, hard look in the mirror before commenting on anyone else's game. None of this seemed to faze Nate. Instead, he slotted in really well, scoring a typical poacher's goal either side of the half-time whistle and over the coming weeks he would become a key player to help the team progress in their league table. Nate loved it as he was spending time with his busy dad and he seemed to be finding his form again, unlike dad who was struggling - much to the enjoyment of his son.

In their first outing, Tony managed an own goal, which, to this day, he still claims was not of his own doing; plus, no matter how hard he tried, he just couldn't keep up with the pace required for effective tackling. Couple that with the lack of interest in him during team selection, as he was nowhere in the mix, and you're left with a broken man battling with his own emotions, trying not to be disheartened with this constant rejection of being left out in the cold as a bench warmer.

Putting his ego aside for a minute, the plan worked really well. They enjoyed some much needed father and son time and to top it all off, Nate's confidence and love of the game was fully restored. Before they knew it, their ten weeks were up and although Nate's presence had made a lasting impression, their services were now surplus to requirements. The church team lived to fight another day in the same league and their regular players gradually returned to duty.

On their final evening, the two of them grabbed a table at a local diner and sat down to a feast of gourmet burger and chips. It was a really good evening with both of them feeling relaxed and just enjoying the moment. Tony looked at his boy and felt a real sense of pride for the way he was developing as a young man.

As the meal ended and coffees were served, he began to share a story of a stifled dream that he hadn't shared for many years. As a teenager, Tony had had a chance encounter at a charity football event, with an inspiring raconteur by the name of Brian Hawkson. Brian had spent the evening with an eager group of captivated youths re-telling stories of old; his experience in WW2, his time helping rebuild his home town, post war, and the trials and tribulations of running a non-league football club in the late 1940's. You see, Brian had always dreamt of taking his precious team, against all odds, on a giant-killing cup run all the way to finally lifting the famous FA Cup. The dream had never been fulfilled but the man's desire and passion to continue had never left his side.

Brian's burning passion to cheer his team on to glory had left a lasting impression on the amiable young Tony and had instilled a seed within him that had taken root. It was as if, at that very moment, the baton had passed hands and the vision of a team stepping out onto a manicured pitch ready for action had become his responsibility. A responsibility that would often haunt his slumber and sometimes leave him daydreaming for hours on end about his own burning desire to lead a band of men towards the twin towers of Wembley stadium. Of course his dream had been cast aside, many a time, throughout most of his adult life and been replaced with the daily grind of a routine existence. Things like building an empire of fully equipped and trained sales consultants as well as providing for, and making time for his family. But every now and then he would permit the dream a brief audience and allow it to aimlessly drift subconsciously through his mind and re-appear in the form of freshly manicured wet turf being torn up by men wholeheartedly committed in a tackle which in turn emanates a dewy petrichor that consumes the nostrils with a bygone era of footballing legends.

For Tony, the last month or so playing six-a-side had caused this dream within to resurface all over again and maybe, just maybe, he thought to himself, now would be the time to pursue and chase down whatever this vision was as it continued to play-out, much the same as a movie trailer, in his mind. And Nate, like his dad all those years ago, found himself awestruck by the tale and felt sure that knowing his father like he did that his lifestyle of procrastination would eventually be won over, finally allowing this gem of a buried dream to surface and finally demand its 15 minutes of fame..

2

The fun sucker of Handley Park

Mike Phillips, head coach of Handley Park Rangers, was one of life's grumpy old men, a dyed-in-the-wool character who believed he knew just about everything there was to know about football and while we're at it, life for that matter. His de-facto philosophy, what you might call "the book of life according to Mike Phillips;" was that life owed him and had never quite delivered. In fact he felt short changed from the cards he'd been dealt thus far and was definitely not prepared to allow the same to happen to him again in, what were now his twilight years. He would make sure that the deck of cards that life had dealt him were stacked in his favour and that he would be repaid in full for the shortcomings he had experienced in the past. Thankfully his wife had never come round to his way of thinking. Once a beautiful woman, a true ray of sunshine that could light up any room, the years of being downtrodden however, had taken their toll. That said, somehow she'd managed to raise, pretty much single-handedly, two fine sons. Well I say two fine sons; one being the image of his mother in all of her loving and thoughtful ways and the other demonstrating many of the negative attributes his dad possessed. The two brothers rarely engaged with each other as they were both on different planets when it came to life and affairs of the heart. This really upset their mother, although dad truthfully, never even noticed as he was far too busy being miserable. He had no idea just how fortunate he was compared to others; a wonderful wife, two healthy sons and a long and fairly prosperous career in the world of football that he had once truly loved. Problem was Mike had never got over the termination of a contract within the professional football league. He just couldn't let it go, he felt that he had been stabbed in the back by the board, the players and the fans at a crucial time in his tenure as manager and therefore he'd missed out on the chance to rub shoulders with the elite of the footballing world. In his eyes he had literally, overnight, gone from hero to zero and someone had to pay and pay they would. His current club, Handley Park Rangers had taken the brunt of his down trodden, negative drivel along with his wife and pretty much anyone who came in contact with him. Except his two boys. Well, that's not strictly true as he had no time for his first born - he was far too amiable. But his youngest, he possibly had potential especially as he'd shown some football ability and was now keeping goal for Handley Park. Maybe, just maybe his son Darren could be the difference in transforming this bunch of underachieving dimwits into a side that was deserving of someone of Mike's stature.

3

Man on a ledge

Nigel Hawkson, son and heir to the late, great Brian Hawkson, was a man under pressure. He believed his current wife (number 3), now estranged to him, was giving him a difficult time. As far as he was concerned she was spending money like it was going out of fashion and was under the assumption that there would be no tomorrow. These alleged "no tomorrow's" were mounting up and taking their toll on Nigel's credit cards, his loans and overdrafts. She was simply spending money he did not have and he was running out of places to escape to - including the private casino he frequented as his gambling debt, which he saw as no more than a way of letting off steam, was starting to run away with itself. Nigel had already had the friendly chat explaining that the friendliness would soon be replaced with hostility if he didn't bring his account into line soon. His dad's precious coachworks factory that he'd inherited had already been sold and the funds frivolously wasted on his lavish lifestyle. But don't get me wrong - this did not leave him without assets as he still possessed a number of rental properties that were returning a yield, along with a couple of retail shops occupied by long term tenants. But the income enjoyed was like a drop in the ocean compared to the debts being raked up at such an alarming rate. And then there was his late father's beloved Handley Park Rangers which as far as Nigel was concerned, was a liability and something he would have offloaded for a quick buck a long time ago but his late father's will had stipulated that the football club could not be sold off for a fixed period of time. (This arrangement was in the hope that his son would recognise the potential, the opportunities and the family values he, himself had embraced all those years ago)

Fortunately, in just over 12 months the restriction would be lifted and Nigel would be able to do as he saw fit with what he described as his father's final chokehold. The clubhouse and out of date stadium along with the grounds were in dire need of some attention. Alas, Nigel had no intention whatsoever of wasting one penny of his ever decreasing inheritance on such a lost cause. You see Nigel's late father, Brian, had been well loved in his hometown of Handley Park. He had served the community well; firstly as a pilot in WW2 and secondly by building a thriving coachworks that employed a large part of the community since the turn of the war. The established coachworks specialised in the conversion of prestige cars, transforming what was already the ultimate in luxury into what was best described as beyond bespoke. Vehicle bodies were handcrafted in preparation for the running gear. Add to that the handcrafted trimming and fitting out of the vehicles to help create that "made from scratch" one-off car. No longer were there metal on wood frames as all steel bodies were used with stressed skin technology to lighten and give strength. The business, of course, kept Brian extremely busy especially with a growing workforce in excess of 500 staff but he did manage to remain very personable and was known as a generous man that had never turned his back on anyone. His door had always been open and the town had been a better place just for having Brian there. But such charitable characteristics had come at a price as much of his time had been taken up either working long hours at the factory or dealing with some problem or other at his beloved football stadium and this is what had caused the rift with his only son. Many times Brian had reached out to his boy in the hope that they could rekindle that bond they had once shared, after all they were alike in so many ways, especially in appearance but Nigel had emotionally shut down on his dad many years ago especially after the passing of his mother. Since that day Nigel had blamed his dad for her brief illness, he had blamed the town for the pain he was carrying and he had blamed the football club for everything . He had always promised himself one day that the club was going to pay big time for all that had happened to him over the years.

4

The halcyon days of Handley Park Rangers

Handley Park Stadium had once epitomised everything that was good about the town. The club shone as a ray of hope for the people that had suffered many casualties and losses of young men and women during WW2. After returning from the war, a young Brian Hawkson and as many men that he could muster had banded together and formed a small charitable club with the sole purpose of serving the community. Football was its primary focus but many events were held there, with the express aim of uniting a town during a time of rationing, grief (many homes were fatherless) and job insecurity.

The land had been purchased from the local town council for a nominal amount, as in reality it was virtually worthless. You see, back in the summer of September 1944, a V2 rocket (otherwise known as a Doodlebug) had strayed off course and aimlessly hit some derelict buildings narrowly missing a popular housing estate. A warning sign stating "Danger! UXB" had remained in place for best part of a year until eventually, after some gentle persuasion, some army friends of Brian's (the royal engineers) had come along and extracted the fuse from the buried bomb, with the aid of a Crabtree steam discharger. It made for an exciting news story for the town and even made headlines in the nationals.

Once the land was bomb free the men, along with some remaining German POW's, set to work uprooting trees and clearing the site of debris. They used the hard-core from the derelict buildings as a foundation for the newly proposed clubhouse and bar. On the halfway line just in front of what would be the main Grandstand, with central gable that housed enough bleachers to accommodate 1200 fans, was access to the subterranean changing rooms, that had once been utilised as the allotted public Anderson shelter for any town folk that may have been caught out during an air raid. Either side of the entrance to the changing areas sat the home and away dugouts. The pitch, no more than a muddy morass, was to be re-seeded under the watchful eye of the club's newly appointed grounds man Arthur Thompson, son of the late old man Thompson, all in preparation for the club to commence play by January 1947. The workers were under strict guidelines to ensure the pitch was level and free from any marked rigs or ruts, in the hope that there would be no future drainage problems that could cause flooding. Behind the Hawker Tempest stand were layers of precarious ash and cinder banks that had to be strengthened and stepped with railway sleepers which, later down the line, were used as makeshift seats by stragglers that were short of the 5d Match day entrance fee. The ethos evoked by the club was steeped in nostalgia inspired by the memories of the many friends and relatives that had fallen during both wars. The club's motto

"Deo iuvante" (with God's help) was etched proudly into the wall by the main entrance.

The clubs nickname, "the Home Guard", was adopted in memory

of old man Thompson, late father of the clubs new grounds man. During rationing, he had pretty much fed the entire town single handily from his hillside allotment, where he was often seen on lookout duty, scanning the horizon for the Hun. The club colours? Now that was a different story! The town had been pretty much divided regarding its choice of home kit. You see, the thought of khaki invoked a stark reminder of the young men who had "chased the colour" for king and country and never returned. Instead, many had hoped for a more vibrant colour with a view to looking to a brighter future but, again due to the lack of resources, unwanted battle dress uniforms had been rounded up and recycled as three quarter length shorts with matching pull-on jersey with hooped white socks. The jerseys were extremely itchy, especially when a player started sweating, and if the heaven's opened, more's the pity for the men as their tops were excellent at harvesting as much rainfall as the leading brand of water butt. That said, not once did those men of pedipulate ability complain, in fact the sense of pride they displayed was a joy and inspiration to the town.

Arguably Bill Shankly's apt description of "the golden triangle of players" - the club, the people and the city coming together as one in unity- best explains the heartbeat of the people of the town. No longer did the club rely on the local cattle to keep the grass on the pitch down to a minimum as it now attracted many a volunteer to not only help steer the horse drawn mower but to also give a hand with just about any duty that would help the club.

However, due to the shortage of men, Brian (just falling short of adopting Press Gang tactics) had to beg, borrow and steal men from neighbouring towns and villages to make up the necessary starting eleven. Over the years and decades that followed, the town took in new settlers to the area from the south, mainly in part due to the coachworks that employed the vast majority of people in the town. In fact, the workforce had doubled from late 1946 through to 1951 and with that came a time of real prosperity. The high street, with its bustling market, extended its territory not only north and south of the town but east and west. Vital services like a doctor's surgery, a dispensing chemist and public library were erected. The town's first public car park with public toilet was located behind the market square, whilst the vast array of independent shops selling local produce were located across the square within a maze of small pedestrian mews.

The clubs first star attraction was a very young, homespun Toddie Tamworth. Although relatively small in stature, boy was Toddie lethal in front of goal. His family had thankfully relocated to Handley Park soon after the war ended as Todd's father had been offered a job as a panel beater at Brian's now thriving coachworks. Todd was one of six siblings, originally from Derbyshire. He first caught the eye of Brian after a charitable fundraiser where soon after the main event, some of the local boys had taken to the pitch for a kick about. Brian had ventured out for some fresh air and ambled across to where the lads were with a view to joining in and letting his hair down a little. But after watching some of Todd's dribbles and ball control he became mesmerised and chose to remain where he was and enjoy watching the lad play. It did not take Brian long to sign Todd to Handley Park, where he would spend the next five seasons terrorizing defences with his rather laid back style of pedipulate play and the growing fan base loved him all the more for it. His name, in fact, still remains on the wall of the club-house amongst the roll call of honour as the clubs top scorer for three seasons running. An achievement that stands to this day. Sadly though, for Brian, the heyday of Handley Park Rangers began to dim when his wife Dora suddenly became ill. Her sickness, although brief, proved to be savage and quickly ravaged her body for all but a few weeks, until finally she could fight no more and reached out to her maker. The rapid decline and sudden loss of Dora was more than Brian could stand. He too lost his zest and taste for life and gradually over the coming months slowly withdrew from not only his business affairs but beloved club as well. His only son, Nigel, who was just like his mother in so many ways, was a remarkable young lad. He was so proud of his dad and the way everyone respected him and he doted on the affections of his mother. But in an instant all that changed when she died. He now had no more than contempt for his father and his precious club. As far as he was concerned, they were to blame for the loss of his mum and no one was going to change the way he felt. A year after the loss of Dora, Nigel, at his own request, was sent to a boarding school. It was yet another blow for Brian but under the circumstances he thought it was for the best and so acquiesced to his son. After that, Brian pretty much became a recluse and only ever heard from his son when he was low on funds, which did rather concern Brian as his boy had seemed to have acquired rather extravagant tastes. And as for Handley Park Rangers? A place that had given so much joy to the people of the town, it soon fell into disrepair and became like a ship without a rudder. A place where so many hopes and dreams had been shared but soon forgotten. It would surely take a miracle for the place ever to recover.

5

Adios amigo to Mike Phillips

Eight games into the new season and Handley Park Rangers were floundering at the bottom of their Tier 8 league table. Six straight defeats, mostly at home, and two goalless draws showing a grand total of 2 miserable points from a possible 24. Mike shook his head in disbelief at the results, he remembered back to the day when his team secured promotion into the football league proper. There had been celebrations well into the night and all of the local and regional press had fought for a brief interview from the man that had gained promotion into the professional football league. But now all Mike could see were a bunch of lazy no hopers who were starting to tarnish his name and reputation and it was starting to grate on him. How dare the local press accuse the likes of "Mike Phillips" of lacking the tactical ability, aptitude and know-how on how to steady the ship of this flagging League 8 side? He stopped and stared aimlessly around the room for a minute and pondered the thought "maybe, just maybe they could be right" but he soon dismissed the thought as no more than baloney. Mike Phillips was, no Mike Phillips is a name to be proud of in the footballing fraternity and the fans and club officials perhaps needed reminding of this fact. Mike let out a deep sigh, closed his old, battered briefcase and headed for the door. He looked around at the damp, death by magnolia walls; he was tired of this club that seemed to be going nowhere fast. He believed, no, he deserved more respect around here.

Little did Mike know that in less than an hour he would be surrounded by paramedics in the back of an ambulance, being rushed through the drive-time traffic of Handley Park to the local hospital. You see, the inner turmoil that had been bubbling below the surface of Mike's turbulent lifestyle had come home to roost in the form of a heart attack. He hadn't even made it to his car before his unconscious body had hit the deck. An off duty steward had found him slumped against a dwarf wall by the turnstiles and had raised the alarm.

Mike spent a total of 2 months in hospital followed by a further 4-6 months of rehabilitation which, unfortunately, he chose to waste believing he no longer required any assistance in his recuperation. In truth, this was a really sad choice by Mike purely because; one – he was scared and clung on to that fear in order to see him through and secondly he just would not accept an outstretched hand of hope to help him as his pride had gotten in the way a long time ago and so continued the moaning and groaning and negative spill about anything and everyone. So Mike's football days ended there, in total misery and anguish about a game that had turned its back on him many years ago and which he still just couldn't let go.

6

Keep calm and carry on

The sudden exit of Mike Phillips created yet another problem for Nigel. He'd been in secret negotiations with a potential buyer for some time and the offer on the table was way more than he'd anticipated. All he needed to do was keep the club at its current league 8 status. He had to avoid relegation at all costs but the club had been rooted to the bottom of the league for best part of the season. Mike had switched onto autopilot a long time ago and had shown no interest in finishing strong as a coach. Instead he'd become known as the "scarlet pimpernel" of Handley Park Rangers, rarely attending training sessions or pre-match warm-ups. He literally ambled out onto the park and sat in his dug out, occasionally making an appearance in the technical area. Nigel and Mike had exchanged many a heated discussion regarding the team's performance, or lack of it, but there was no getting through to Mike. They were on different paths; Mike just wanted out of football so he could fine tune his moaning skills elsewhere and Nigel needed to offload this inherited asset if he was to have any chance of remaining financially solvent. Mike had received his wish of exiting football and as expected in rather doom and gloom circumstances, whilst Nigel was hoping he'd receive his wish of erasing Handley Park Rangers from the face of the earth. Now without a manager (even if it was only in body and not in spirit) the club would disappear into the obscurity of Level 9 football, which meant a hefty dent in his already depleted net worth and he was not prepared to accept that. A replacement was required, sooner, rather than later but attracting a manager with some form of pedigree was virtually impossible. There was no money to entice with, no perks or benefits, no status or prospects, well that's how Nigel saw it anyway. He poured himself an early Scotch whisky. He seemed to be breaking his unwritten rule of not before midday more frequently these days, but today he needed it. He was so close to sealing his deal. He knew that the long term goal of the would-be-owners was to demolish the club and build "affordable living accommodation" but the deal would surely be blocked if such information were to come to light locally, so for now Nigel would keep schtum. He would make out that everything was fine and dandy; that a manager of high calibre would soon be at the helm with a view to steering the club out of the relegation zone and beyond. "Yes that was the plan", Nigel thought to himself. "Let's just keep calm and carry on."

"Jolly good idea," he declared to no one in particular as he reached for his rather over laden glass tumbler. "So where do I find this bod? I must put out some feelers, perhaps that Hayworth chap might know of a name or two," he said to himself again. And with that he returned to his rather taxing crossword which was always good at helping him ease into the day.

7

Radio Interview between Charles Hayworth; HP "Live on air" radio and Nigel Hawkson HPR owner.

Charles: "Thanks Mr. Hawkson for the impromptu visit today. You're live on air with HP radio. Losing your man at the helm so suddenly must have come as a bit of a blow for the club."

Nigel; "Yes thanks Charles. Losing such an important figure for the club is a challenge but no one person is bigger than our club. Our thoughts are with Mike and his family right now and we wish him a speedy recovery".

Charles: "So what now Nigel? Are you looking for young blood or somebody tried and tested to steady the ship?"

Nigel: "Yes steady the ship. I rather like that. Don't suppose you are free Charles are you?" Nigel states laughing!

Charles: slightly embarrassed but as always ready with a comeback. "No 'fraid not Nigel but perhaps it might be a good time for you to consider stepping up to the plate yourself!"

Nigel: considering his next move. "Running a non-league

football club is a very complex thing with lots to consider. You ever tried it Charles?" declares Nigel tongue in cheek.

Charles: "No you're right. I'm sure it's taxing Nigel although wasn't it Len Shackleton who wrote a chapter in his memoirs, The Clown Prince of Soccer about the average Director's knowledge of Football and left a single page blank?

Nigel looked at Charles belligerently as if he was about to give birth to a reindeer. He stood up, dusted himself down, straightened his tie and pronounced; "this conversation is over" and walked out of the studio.

Charles; "Well folks, that was the infamous Nigel Hawkson enlightening us all on the future of our beloved Handley Park Rangers."

8

Sowing a seed

Nate, as usual, was running late. He'd agreed to meet the lads on the 3G to play "cuppies" prior to Thursday night training but had got caught up with some friends in a heated debate about the sudden departure of the first Premiership coach relieved of his duties this season. The Premiership was only 8 games into the season's fixtures and a second International break was about to commence. The League champions were floundering just above the relegation zone and just could not seem to kick start their season, whilst two of the three newly promoted clubs had got off to a flying start, claiming at least two high flying scalps apiece along the way. The friends were split between who should have gone first. The current run of form seemed to put another coach in the spotlight as a potential candidate for the firing squad, especially as his team were yet to win a game at home.

Nate's coach shot him a look of disapproval as he threw his sport's bag on the bench and quickly stripped his jogging bottoms off. With a quick "sorry coach" Nate rushed out onto the pitch and joined his teammates, who were already performing warm-up exercises. After their 15 minutes of intensive stretches, the players grabbed bibs and prepared for passing drills followed by shots at goal before finishing their session with a kick about. Nate's team, the red bibs, managed to steal a goal in the last minute giving them victory and after some friendly banter, the lads sat on the 3G surface to discuss this weekend's clash with the team who were currently 1 point below them in the league. As per the norm, Nate's dad was standing by the perimeter fence deep in conversation with one of the dads. They were engrossed, talking about the shock departure of Mike Phillips and Tony was trying to come up with a list of possible solutions for a possible replacement. Tony had always kept an eye on the form and the results of Handley Park ever since his chance encounter with the great man Brian Hawkson and as he began to share this story, he noticed the other dad's demeanour change as he hastily brought the conversation to a close with a view to going their own separate ways.

Nate stood in front of the two men, his dad and the other dad who he now recognised as Nigel. He knew him through his estranged son; Todd, in fact he'd been out to a few fancy restaurants with them over the years but had never really struck up a conversation with Nigel. He knew he was kind of a high flyer in the town and owned a number of properties as well as Handley Park Rangers. He wasn't really a stay at home dad, more of an aloof dad who preferred sitting on the fringes of his son's daily life. As he watched the two men awkwardly finish their conversation a thought dropped into his mind about his dad's dream. Before he knew it he found himself, rather excitedly, propositioning Nigel with this rather half-cocked idea about his dad taking over as the new manager of HPR. It didn't stop there as he went on about how great his dad was with running a local youth team and how he had inspired the lads not just in how they played their football but how he had impacted some of their private lives with helpful life skills. The initial response from both men was one of bewilderment, soon to be followed by a nervous laughter which kind of embarrassed Nate.

Later in the car, Tony apologised to his boy for his nonplussed reaction but also thanked him for "putting it out there" as when it came to Tony's secret ambition, Nate had achieved more in a few weeks than Tony had in over 20 years. That said, Tony doubted himself far too easily when it came to following this lifelong dream; if only he could pass the idea on to someone else as he was beginning to tire of it all.

9

An unsuspecting marionette to fill the void

It was early and Nigel could not sleep; he'd been restless for most of the night, tossing and turning about the stresses and strains he was going through at the moment. He just couldn't seem to find any peace or serenity right now. Thoughts had been rushing through his rather chaotic mind throughout the night including faded memories of his late father; why was it that people had regarded him with such high esteem and yet Nigel was treated with contempt? (Or so it seemed) Surely people should realise just how much he contributes to the local community?   But instead, people like the Charles Hayworths of this world seem to think they can boss him around. Well, that would have to stop. Finally, feeling rather agitated, he got out of bed and headed to the kitchen where he poured himself a rather large dram of Scotch whisky into his steaming hot cup of coffee. The norm these days was to wake up jaded and bleary eyed, which was always a prerequisite for a foul mood. But that did not matter anyway, as there was never anyone around to share his mood with. Both his wife and son remained estranged to him, unless of course, they needed something, which they rarely did these days. There was a bit of time spent with his son Todd after training but that invariably turned into a slanging match, purely because they just did not understand each other. Not like "old Mr. He-who-can-do-no-wrong" and his annoying son Nate. They were always deep in conversation or bear hugging and doing high fives. It made Nigel sick to the core at such an unnecessary expression of emotion, especially in public for all to see; just wasn't right!

There had been a time, as a small child when he would have loved that kind of open affection from his dad but the opportunity never presented itself. So Nigel had slowly, over time, taught himself, whilst at boarding school, to stifle and restrict his emotions which of course continued throughout his school years, closely followed by his teenage years, moving on to full time adulthood including all of his marriages.

He had never really shared what was on his mind and thinking about it, he'd never actually shared his inner thoughts with another human being. Initially he thought what he had to say had no value. It didn't matter now though as he was so caught up in his own twisted, pent up pain and anguish. It just seemed to boil up from his very being pretty much at will these days and there appeared to be nothing he could do about it. Well, that's not exactly true. He could anaesthetize the feelings with booze sometimes until, it seemed, his back teeth were floating. But whatever it took, he would do it, just to get him through this transitional period of offloading this dump of a football club.

As Nigel finished the dregs of his coffee, a thought appeared in his hazy mind. That dad. The annoying one with the brat of a son; could he be the one that would keep the club in league 8?

34

After all, you only needed a pulse to improve on the work Mike had performed. But the real motive was starting to take shape; could he, Nigel, convince all those concerned with the welfare of the club, that this clean shaven, whiter than white character could generate some results to keep the club buoyant? If so, then maybe, given time, Tony could prove to have been the catalyst that would send the club into a freefall of poor results and financial ruin; especially if Nigel were to invest a little bit of time in steering the ship towards disaster. The sale of the club would have taken place and Nigel would be a free man. A free man with a couple of quid on the hip and happy in the knowledge he had spearheaded the demise of the club - with a quick character assassination in the form of Tony the scapegoat and all just for kicks! Wow. All in a day's work. A day's work! "Can't be bad!" Nigel thought to himself. "Now how can I initiate a discussion with the mark", he said out loud to no one in particular. The brat, he thought with that ridiculous story about leading a group of men to glory. Nigel grabbed his mobile and began calling his son. Perhaps a cosy meal was in order for him and his son; oh and he must invite his friend Nate. Well at least he'd help stop the arguing, at least for now anyway.

10

Big Mac – the dark horse of HPR

You could easily pass by Handley Park's number 2, Billy McGrath, without noticing him. He had that covert look about him that made him seem inconsequential and yet he was a very profound man. If you wanted to converse with him, it would be up to you to initiate. To begin with, the preliminaries were always difficult, a bit like pulling hen's teeth but once you passed his acid test of "worth talking to" then he would open up and become animated about your discussion and what you had to say. He possessed a rather rare virtue of being able to make you feel comfortable, important and valued all at once. He listened intently and before you knew it, you would have disclosed way more about the going-ons in your world than you would ever have felt comfortable doing.

Whilst Nigel would never let Billy, or "Big Mac" as he was affectionately known, darken-his-door (he had no time for him), Mike on the other hand had always maintained the greatest respect and admiration for him; partly because of his tactical ability but mainly due to the fact that he was scared of Billy. You see Billy was ex-army but not just any unit; he was special-forces and had been for fifteen years of his life. That was until he'd taken early retirement due to a behind-enemy-lines altercation with some obscure rebel forces in the Egyptian desert. Not the sort of everyday occurrence for you and me, but all in a day's work for Billy and that is all that you would get out of him, nothing more! And so a legend had been born at Handley Park Rangers, with the mysterious story growing in stature year on year due to the reticence of its owner.

But in essence, Billy was a salt of the earth man who had a real passion for Handley Park and the people of Handley Park. He had grown to love them both over the years but had always felt disappointed for them, especially with the growth of the club. He'd always felt the club had been let down by Mike's attitude and by Nigel's lack of interest; you see, Billy had always felt that he could do something really special here with the team, if only it could be managed and guided by someone who had the same passion and love that he held so dearly. As things stood, Big Mac believed that the writing was on the wall for the old place; no manager, an aloof owner who was well out of his depth concerning business affairs and no money. He didn't think it would be long before the doors were closed, the turn style rotated for the last time to let the good old British public in and the club sold to the highest bidder - all of which he felt sure would have left old-man Hawkson turning in his grave.

Since the shock departure of Mike, Nigel had remained pretty much incommunicado whilst Billy had kept the squad together. Well at least that was something. There were 12 remaining fixtures before the end of the season and the club still remained rooted to the bottom of their division. There appeared to be no way out of the relegation zone and tier 9 football looked inevitable for the lads. Morale had always been an issue under Mike but at present it was at an all time low. Just getting through the next 12 games with nothing but damage limitation on their minds seemed to be the order of the day. Other than that, there was little or no expectation from the squad. This crushed the likes of Billy, as he truly believed in the ability of his players, except Darren, the clubs languid goalkeeper and captain - now there was a difficult-to-love character if ever there was one! He couldn't keep goal for toffee and seemed to take great pleasure in abusing, at will, his defence as and when he saw fit. As far as he was concerned, the rake of goals conceded this season had been down to defensive errors, and not his lack of ability to keep goal. As his father happened to be Mike Phillips the manager (or now ex-manager) he believed he was accountable to no man, which showed both on and off the pitch. Billy had always relished the opportunity to challenge Darren's behaviour, but Mike had always made him a no go zone so Darren had been allowed to continue his ugly behaviour amongst the players. This had caused havoc in the dressing room for Billy just to calm down the players and avert their anger. But now with Mike being gone, surely *that* would have made Darren feel vulnerable but instead it seemed to have the adverse effect on him - he seemed to increase the insults and foul language towards his teammates. Something had to be done about Darren Phillips and soon. Billy feared that he would have a mutiny on his hands and that was the last thing this fledgling team needed right now.

11

(The rear view mirror)

Todd seemed to take great pleasure in twisting the knife into his dad when it came to their relationship; he just couldn't help himself. This made things really uncomfortable for Nate, as being in a public place did not seem to faze either one of them when it came to expressing how they felt. It was like being in a war zone with both sides hurling insults and accusations at will and with no obvious let up for those sitting in no-man's-land - which happened to be Nate on this occasion. Nigel looked jaded and smelt like a brewery and seemed pre-occupied with his thoughts - giving the impression that he wasn't really in the room, which of course fuelled Todd even more. Nate just wished that they could both call a truce and start over; yes, maybe Nigel was a bit of a let-down when it came to his fatherly duties but Todd also played his part by constantly making sure his dad paid for his misdemeanours over and over and over again. No one was going to win this battle – no one.

The restaurant chosen by Nigel embraced his typical swanky look, complete with nouvelle cuisine that was hard to pronounce and always left you hungry for more. That kind of food was always wasted on the two young men who were far more interested in a good old fashioned burger and chips! They sat in silence through most of the meal with the only break in silence coming from their waitress asking the customary "is everything fine with your meal?" followed by approving nods and nothing more. Once their plates were cleared, Nigel attempted to open the conversation again, but this time with a different tact. He asked after Nate's dad; how he was; how his business was doing, you know, the usual surface small talk which eventually led to the question he really wanted to ask. "Tell me Nate, do you think your dad may have some spare time to assist with managerial duties regarding the squad? On a short term basis, of course". "Just while I look at all of the possible, managerial candidates, that I have on the table." (which totalled a big fat zero at the last count).

Nate tried to hide his enthusiasm as he nonchalantly nodded his head and said that he would mention it to his dad (knowing full well that he would crash through the door at home in excitement to tell his dad). Nate thought he did rather well trying to conceal his elation but Nigel, like a seasoned poker player, observed what he needed to and could tell by the look in the young man's eyes that he had him; hook, line and sinker.

Soon after, Nigel settled the bill and followed the boys out into the car park. It was a typically cold winter's night with leaves still swirling in the air and a fine misty rain that always seemed, for no apparent reason, to make people frown. Nigel waved goodbye to the boys and jumped behind the wheel of his Daimler. He looked at himself in the rear view mirror; he just didn't seem to recognise himself these days and he didn't like the reflection looking back at him. He felt tired and exhausted for what was really no apparent reason. In fact he sensed that all was not well concerning his health, as he just did not feel right. Work wasn't exactly taxing; in fact his work rate these days was so lacking that he felt that he had very little to offer in the way of business acumen or industry know-how. He felt pretty useless and that is why, truth be told, he hated himself and what he had become. He left quite a trail of destruction in his wake; two divorces and a soon to be third and a teenage son who hated being in the same county as him, let alone room. "Is this all that life really has to offer?" he thought to himself, "there has to be more than this". He smashed his hand down on to his walnut veneered steering wheel and shook himself. Why did his boy always make him feel so inadequate after they'd met, what was the hold on him? He'd done nothing wrong other than provide a state-of-the-art family home with all the modcons along with a private education and generous allowance. Most people would have given their right arm for such a privilege but not Todd. No, he'd done nothing but throw it all back in his father's face and with such venom! Nigel took a second look in the rear view mirror now a bit more composed. "I'm the victim here ,"he thought to himself, "what has a man got to do to be shown some respect around here? That's more like it," Nigel thought to himself as his social facade returned and his emotions were now back in check.

Now let's see what his new pawn Nate can come up with. Nigel would leave it a few days and no more before he would call Tony directly and invite him in for coffee. "We'll see," he thought as he pushed his car's ignition button which powered his V6 twin turbo engine into life. The sound emitted from the exhaust of Nigel's car always gave him such pleasure. He checked his rearview mirror for the last time and pulled his car out of the restaurant's car park. "You know," he thought to himself "it might not be such a bad idea to ease up on the booze for a time."

He *did* feel tired and he needed to be sharp and alert if he was to pull everything together concerning Handley Park Rangers, especially if he wanted to maximise his return on investment and, after all, that is what it was all about. Wasn't it?

12

It's time to throw in the towel

Big Mac didn't need to scan the dwindling crowd or the over stretched regular faces of volunteers to establish that Nigel had yet again not bothered to show his face in support of his soon-to-be-tier 9 non-league football club. In fact, he could not remember the last time he had seen Nigel at a home game. More's the pity, as right now the club was rudderless and in desperate need of some leadership. Mac was just about ready to throw in the towel.

It was a typical, midweek, wet and windy wintry night. The floodlights were just about doing enough to illuminate the pitch, purely because they were in dire need of an overhaul. But as Mac knew of no local electrician that he could pull a favour with (in fact he was flat broke when it came to pulling in favours), he was left with the only option of "making do" and "making do" was starting to tick him off right now. He was "making do" with a club on the verge of bankruptcy, he was "making do" with a bunch of de-motivated, talented lads who currently couldn't kick a ball for toffee and he was "making do" with an owner who just couldn't care less. "One more game is all I will give," he promised himself as he sat back in his Ply lined, DIY makeshift, pillar-box-red dugout. They were 10 minutes into the second half and already trailing by 3 goals to nil. He was hoarse from screaming constant reminders of tactical defensive play that was not being met, coupled with silly school boy errors resulted in yet another goalmouth scramble.

Mac had always prided himself on his youthful looks and outward demeanour but tonight, he really felt his 50 something age and much like the dimly lit Handley Park floodlights, he sensed the brightness starting to dim from his eyes. He was woken from his reverie by the foul mouthed rant of his least favourite player; Darren Phillips. Now, there was someone high on the punch-o-meter! You see, Darren knew it all and firmly believed that there was nothing worth knowing that he didn't know already. For almost two seasons now he had bullied, no sorry I mean captained, this team into submission and to be quite frank, he was despised by his teammates all bar one. He had one ally - a central defensive player; a guy named Frank Malone. Now Frank was from the same mould as Darren; but instead of utilising his limited vocabulary that originated from the sewer, he much preferred to get physical and he really wasn't too fussed whether it was one of his own or the opposing team. Either way, he liked to let his fists do the talking, or if not, a late into the game, off the ball dirty tackle just to give him a fighting chance of lasting the full 90 minutes - which was pretty much a rarity these days.

With 15 minutes to go, the ref blew for a free-kick just outside of the Handley Park Ranger's penalty box - all thanks to Frank's impressive, late sliding tackle that had completely sideswiped an attacking player. He was now being nursed by a physio as he was showing signs of concussion but of course, there was no remorse from Frank. He just rounded the ref, ready for an outburst, as he was shown a red card and told to leave the field of play. The proceedings were soon followed by 4 or 5 Handley players having to help escort Frank from the field, coupled with the abusive undertones from Darren, just for good measure. Big Mac held his head in his hands, totally ashamed by the whole debacle; he gave Frank a scathing look as he passed by the dugout, heading for an early bath. Eventually, the forthcoming free kick produced a number of rebounds, creating mayhem in the six yard box, before a cheap goal was conceded from somebody's shin, or shoulder, or arm- you just couldn't tell with the amount of bodies languishing on the goal line.

After that, Handley Park pretty much let the opposing team keep possession of the ball in order to run the clock down. No Fergie-time was required here tonight as the home team were just desperate to get off the field of play and put tonight behind them after such a humiliation. The lads sat in their makeshift dressing room, a Portakabin leased on a temporary basis some 4 years prior. It had only meant to be a stop-gap whilst their changing room was renovated but since work had stopped due to the discovery of Asbestos, no tradesman had returned. The tin can of a dressing room was freezing and provided no adequate shower-ing unless you were prepared to dance naked, screaming for mercy under a shower head that provided lashings and lashings of frozen water.

The team results were starting to take their toll; defeat after defeat seemed to have crushed their morale as any hope they'd been hanging on to had long since departed. You'd have thought with Mike gone, a new lease of life would have instilled some sort of confidence within the players. But it was as if they were stuck on Mike's imaginary bus of negativity and they did not know how to get off. If you wanted a tactician extraordinaire, then Mac was your man but lifting chins off the ground just wasn't his bag and so the team just sat there in silence. You could sense that they had all come to the end of the road; even the unsavoury Darren had nothing to say. "One more game", Mac thought to himself" one more and that's it. I'm gone" which was pretty much what the rest of the players were thinking, especially as three in the last month had already jumped ship. It was as if the request for "women and children first" had already been declared on their stricken vessel and the final call of "everyman for himself" was about to be announced anytime soon. Mac knew it; the players knew it; the only one who didn't was Nigel... probably because he had abandoned ship some time ago.

13

The big chap between the sticks

Nate could not contain himself as he burst through the door at home. He was desperate to tell his dad about his evening (minus the bickering between Nigel and Todd of course). "What an opportunity for dad," Nate thought "but I wonder what Nigel meant by 'assist with managerial duties'? Will Nigel be running the team? Surely not," he thought to himself "that's a little beneath him, especially as he shows very little interest in the club these days." He rushed upstairs in search of his dad nearly knocking his mum over in the process. She told him to calm down and share what was on his mind. There wasn't time, where was dad? But he soon realised dad wasn't in as at the last minute he'd agreed to make up numbers in his firm's 6-a-side team. So Nate sat on the stairs and told his mum about this evening - about dad's dream (he was unsure if she knew) and about how Nigel had asked Nate if he thought his dad could help out. Nate's mum was aware of Tony's ambition; that one went way back to when they had first started courting but her thoughts were focused elsewhere. She didn't trust that Nigel Hawkson; there was always an ulterior motive where that man was concerned.

She couldn't put her finger on it but knew he was up to something and that it would not be to the benefit of anyone except himself. Helen decided to keep her thoughts to herself especially as she looked up at her son and could see how animated he was about the whole thing. So she just encouraged him, stating that she was sure his dad would be thrilled about the opportunity and looked forward to Nate sharing the news with him;
that was assuming he managed to get home in one piece.

Earlier in the evening Helen and Tony had had one of their rare heated exchange of words. She had dared to accuse him of swimming down that long river in Egypt called denial (The Nile), stating that he was no longer the spring chicken he once was and may find it hard to keep up with the pace of Power League football. He hadn't taken it well. This was confirmed when he left the house in a huff with his cheap, out of date Astro Turf trainers on the wrong feet, so she decided to let him figure that one out for himself as he slammed the front door and headed for the car. Although he wouldn't admit it, Tony had sulked virtually the entire 25 minute journey across town. "No spring chicken" how dare she accuse me of not keeping up with the pace? "I've still got it, I'm not sure what it really is but hey, who's counting?" "I'll show her," he thought to himself. He swung his legs out of the driver's seat and bent forward to tighten his laces and soon realised that his trainers were on the wrong feet. He laughed to himself; "I bet she spotted my mistake," and laughed again but at himself this time.

He stretched and started slowly jogging over to the other players, joining them in their gentle exercise as they warmed up and discussed the game in hand. Their opponents were a bunch of newcomers who'd recently joined their league so they had no kit and were playing in bibs. The lads ventured out onto the pitch and practised passing and shots at goal. Tony looked over at his opponents and in doing so he spotted their keeper. He was a big chap he thought to himself, he must have been 6' 7", maybe a little more and he looked as strong as an ox. Not all pumped up from weights but naturally solid. The two of them exchanged glances and nodded to one another.

The guys left the field and huddled to discuss their game plan, which seemed pretty basic to Tony. Their remit seemed to be - pass the ball to Jonathon and let him do the rest. But none of this really mattered as Tony soon discovered that he was to start the game on the sidelines and that if he was required he would be called for. Not a good start for his ego but he wasn't going to hold that against them (he'd already done that with his wife). They kicked off and Tony's team (Invictus) took the game to the opposition early in the hope of a quick goal. But the opposing side's defence, did a pretty good job of soaking up the pressure and seemed happy with this tactic, hoping to stage a counter attack when the time was right. And sure enough! When the opportunity presented itself, one of the opposing players just broke out of defence and sprinted away from all 10 players towards goal and with a slight drop of his shoulder, rounded the goalie and tapped the ball into the net.

The Invictus players were livid and openly blamed each other for their lack of concentration; after all, these games were taken seriously and were often treated as do or die situations. After the shock goal, the squad re-grouped and figuratively speaking took the gloves off and went to the mattresses (a little known Chicago gangster term) as an act of war. There would be no mercy as they set out to humiliate and destroy their opponents with shock and awe tactics. But their efforts were futile as the defence held firm, waiting for their next counter, which of course soon arrived in the form of a stunning throw by the keeper. He just launched the ball so clinically, almost like an NFL quarterback, straight to the chest of his striker who proceeded to bring the ball under control and again round the keeper finishing with a tap in goal. Tony, no more than a mere spectator, watched in awe as his seasoned team were dismantled and overrun completely at will by this unknown side. He found the whole experience fascinating as he watched the build up play of his opponents. It was so simplistic in its form but very effective play. Tony's team mates soon looked ready to throw in the towel and concede defeat until they were awarded a cheap penalty, gifted them after a defender's hand was caught with the ball in the penalty area. A 2-1 defeat for Invictus would have been far more palatable for them, bearing in mind the penalty awarded was against the run of play. Their main man Jonathon swaggered up to the plate, grabbed the ball and looked to psych out the man mountain in goal; which can be a little difficult to do when you have to lift your gaze by 12". Jonathon placed the ball on the penalty spot, moved an outstretched pointed finger goal bound and turned his back heading at least 20 yards in preparation for his run up. He nonchalantly placed his hands on his hips, adjusted his stance and focused. He really wanted this goal and no one was going to stop him, not even the Sasquatch lookalike that stood between him and glory road. Although Jonathon may have lacked a little in stature, he soon made up for it in the form of a rocket of a left foot which he used to good effect. It seemed like an age had passed before Jonathon finally launched himself towards the ball; he was like a blur as he passed his teammates heading for the static ball. Interestingly enough, Tony noticed that the goalie hadn't moved once during the shenanigans and play acting that took place. He just looked squarely ahead at the ball. Thud! The ball was impacted by Jonathon's designer coloured left boot, heading top corner. Game over! But no, not tonight and to this day Tony still can't fathom how the goalie did it. It was as if he seemed to discreetly adjust his stance effortlessly in preparation to meet the ball and not only that; he saved it with both hands catching it rather than parrying it across goal. Everyone, bar Tony it seemed, missed this miraculous moment purely because there was no spectacular dive, just a practical, decisive movement between the sticks.

The final whistle blew immediately after the shot and the teams shook hands congratulating and consoling both at the same time. Tony made his way out onto the pitch to commiserate with his team but more importantly he had to speak with that goalie. A minute or so passed as Tony's team discussed where it had all gone wrong and who was to blame for this unexpected defeat. By rights, Tony should have been a little disappointed with not being brought on as a sub, if anything just to appease his ego. But to be honest, he was far more interested in speaking with that goalie and before long, his wish was granted as the glow of the floodlights disappeared behind the man who stood before him.

14

A rather big piece of the jigsaw puzzle

Tony looked up, shielding his eyes from the glow of the flood-lights and met, for the very first time, the uncertain gaze of Clay Jackson. Sure Clay was a freakishly large man. After all, he must have been 6' 7", maybe even taller, with a clearly defined upper body torso with anvil shaped biceps all complete with powerful legs that any athlete would be proud of. But he also possessed the simplest and kindest eyes that perhaps Tony had ever encountered. You see, Clay was what the world would class as a 'simpleton', someone frivolously described as "a sandwich short of a picnic" but surprisingly, unbeknown to most, this man had real depth of wisdom and knowledge. He had so much to offer but had never really been allowed or entrusted with the oppor-tunity to make good on his destiny. You see Clay, without realising it, was a man on a mission. His goal in life was to encourage and nurture and offer words of encouragement to just about anyone he met along the way. In fact, Clay was the kind of guy that would always see the best in someone, never their shortcomings. He was always keen to impart some of his wisdom or an inspiring quote to encourage or nurture that person but, truth be told, those kind words of wisdom would, 9 times out of 10, fall on deaf ears. Problem was that it was so easy to be impressed with Clay's outward appearance but as soon as someone engaged in discourse with him, they would soon switch off, mainly due to his long drawn out cumbersome conversations steeped in a deep southern American twang that tended to accentuate a kind of clumsiness. If only people would take the time to get to know the, quite frankly, amazing man he truly was. Tony took the time to overlook what some would describe as Clay's shortcomings and instead focused on what the man had to say. Sure enough, it left him encouraged, upbeat and downright positive as well as a little lighter which came as a complete surprise to him. He was impressed, really impressed with this guy and felt sure that their paths had crossed for a specific reason but for now he had no clue as to what purpose. Either way, he let Clay know how impressed he was with his understated style of keeping goal. Clay, of course, played the compliment down as no more than a fortunate run of play, but Tony knew better. The brief encounter ended there with both men going their separate ways but not before looking over one last time at each other and giving a gentle sideways nod of respect and admiration knowing that sooner or later that their paths would cross again.

Tony jumped in his car and left for home; he had turned down the chance of a quick pint with his team mates as he was keen to get home to Helen and make amends. His brief encounter with Clay had soon put paid to his disagreement with Helen and had given him a little perspective on things and made him think of her and how much he loved and appreciated her. He even stopped and grabbed some flowers and chocolates before reaching home, which totally confused Helen as he came through the door. This was unlike Tony to be so impulsive or romantic, especially after a slightly heated tete-a-tete; he normally sulked for an hour or two at the very least before offering some form of olive branch in the hope of disguising the fact that he hated arguing with his wife. Helen already knew this but loved to tease him as she enjoyed the way he struggled when they disagreed. Put him in front of a rowdy audience or throw him in at the deep end of a business consultation and he was your man but in front of the woman he loved he would be at all sixes and sevens. They both sat down to catch up on their day. Helen assumed that Tony's heavy mood would have remained, especially as the team had lost and it was likely he would have remained on the sub's bench but instead, the man before her was upbeat and eager to talk. So the question raised was "Who are you and what have you done with my husband?" He laughed. "I'm not sure," was his response" but I did meet a rather interesting American lad".

"Interesting? How so?" replied Helen, which fell on deaf ears as Nate entered the conservatory looking like he was ready to burst.
 "Dad, you'll never believe it. I met with Todd and Nigel this evening for a meal".

"That must have been challenging based on their track record," Tony chirped in.

"I know dad it was but listen," said Nate "Nigel asked me if you would be interested in helping out with managerial duties at the club, as a kind of interim I guess."

 Tony looked shocked and put his drink down on the coffee table. "Well say something dad, isn't that amazing? What do you think?" Tony looked to Helen, who just shrugged her shoulders and nodded as if to corroborate the story. Tony pushed his chair back and stood up, not quite to his full six foot stature. He aimlessly carried out an unprecedented 360 degree at the table before reaching for his hot chocolate and taking a long gulp. He looked at Helen and Nate again and a large grin suddenly broke out across his face as he could no longer contain the excitement that was building up inside him. Both Helen and Nate pointed and laughed at Tony not only because of the uncontrolled grin across his face but more for him sporting a chocolate moustache that had formed across his top lip after his last slurp of hot chocolate.

"Will you call him dad?" asked Nat.

"Of course son, I will call him tomorrow. Oh, and Nate, thank you," stated Tony.

"For what?" Nate asked

"For believing in me", choked Tony.

"Oh that's easy dad. You just need to believe in yourself a little more."

"I know, I know, "pronounced Tony and sat down to ponder all that was happening right now. He was a processor and liked to take time to work things out in his mind. This, of course, was a positive thing to do but often left him slightly paralysed in thought as he weighed up the pros and cons and the motives of all concerned. This was especially relevant as Helen had previously warned him to be wary of Nigel Hawkson and knowing Helen as he did, he felt sure her intuition would be right. Either way, he would not let this opportunity slip through his hands and so decided to call Nigel in the morning to gauge a better understanding of what he was proposing. His thoughts, once more, turned again to Clay. For some reason he felt connected to this man and could not help but like him, coupled with the fact that he could really keep goal. "That was some penalty save tonight and he made it look so effortless," he thought to himself. "That is a gift and I bet he has more besides," he thought. "We'll see, we'll see."

15

It's time to plan an exit strategy

It wasn't the best of evenings for Nigel. His stress levels would have been through the roof had it not been for the copious amounts of Scotch dulling his senses. He had felt sure he was on a good run as the evening had started so well. At one stage, he was at least £10k up but as the night wore on, so too did his run of cards and before he knew it, his entire bankroll was gone along with his limited line of credit. As he was maxed out, this meant his evening was short lived so he made his way to the bar where he ordered himself a consolation prize of a large port and brandy; just to settle his stomach. As he knocked back his drink and waited for the usual burning sensation to hit the back of his throat, he noticed his phone vibrating on the granite worktop of the bar. He looked to see who was calling, but did not recognise the number, other than the fact that it was a local number. After several persistent rings he picked up. "Hello"

"Hello is that Nigel? It's Tony, Tony Jeffs."

Finally Nigel responded; "Tony who?"

"Oh hello Nigel, its Tony; Nate's dad."

Nigel's hazy mind began to compute the name, trying to place it somewhere until finally he had a match. He thought he said to himself "oh the annoying one," but Tony heard it. He decided to let it ride as he was pretty sure the voice he was listening to seemed slightly slurred. So he continued;

"Is now not a good time Nigel as I can always call tomorrow?"

No response was forthcoming. "Are you okay Nigel?" asked Tony. Continued silence from the other end of the phone. Again Tony spoke "Is there anything I can do for you?"

Finally Nigel spoke "Yes, you can come by the offices tomorrow and we can talk then" and that was his final response, followed by a dead tone humming down the line. It wasn't really what Tony expected but he chose to not let it take the edge off of his cheerful mood and so he returned to Helen and Nate in the lounge making the excuse that now had not been a convenient time to talk. As for Nigel, he soon left the bar and made his way down the stairs, out into the night air but not before passing two rather burly men that, unbeknown to him, were waiting in the wings at the bottom of the stairs. They asked him if he had had a pleasant evening to which he responded that the night was still young. The men did not respond or move aside for that matter but instead intensified the conversation by stepping rather uncomfortably closer. One of them leaned in to let Nigel know that his debt to the casino had now been passed to him and that the terms of the debt were about to take a turn for the worst. Finally adding that he would be in touch soon and to enjoy the rest of his evening. Nigel, rather flustered stepped past them and out into the cold night air. His car was just a few feet away but he knew that he was well over the driving limit and so he headed down into town to grab a cab.

Fifteen minutes later he was on his way home and as he sat in the back seat of the cab he allowed his mind to go over the conversation that had taken place. The question nagging Nigel was whether he had just been threatened because from where he was standing, that's exactly what had just happened. By the time the cab arrived outside his gated home, his stress levels were through the roof! He knew at that very moment that he needed to come up with some kind of self preservation plan maybe? As right now it seemed that things were starting to get a little out of hand.

16

The rough diamond geezer

Sam Ryan had followed the blues since the tender age of 4. His mates had always accused him of being a trophy hunter and not a true blue but truth be told, it did not bother him as he was following in the footsteps of his late father. If the blues were good enough for him, then they were good enough for Sam and he'd continued that ethos well into his late teens and early twenties. Initially with the help of his mum and a part time job, he'd managed to hang on to his father's season ticket, which he'd held so dear to his heart. The seat was just behind the goal at the rowdy end of the stadium; 10 rows back, allowing for a great view of the 6 yard box where, over the years, both Sam and his dad had witnessed many a goalmouth scramble. Sam had even kept his dad's, now threadbare, number 10 shirt, which he had worn not only for sentimental reasons but also because it gave him a sense of belonging amongst the fans as well as making him still feel, in some small way, close to his dad.

Sam had left school as soon as legally permitted, not because he'd disliked school, no he'd made some great mates there who he was sure would last a lifetime. No, the reason was that he'd wanted to pursue the dream his father had often spoke about of him becoming a Pro-footballer. And so Sam took the plunge and committed to a local football academy hoping that one day he would be able to fulfill his late father's ambition for him. Without a shadow of a doubt Sam possessed great football attributes, such as the intelligence to read the game at high tempo as well his heading ability which produced many goal assists during his early academy days. However, after an untimely tackle chasing a 50/50 ball, he suffered a knee ligament injury that required surgery and subsequently put him out of action for six months. Soon after, he experienced the big shock of being released forthwith from the football league academy and that was the end of that. Sam was devastated, the rejection was too much for him to handle at such a young age and he struggled to shake it off. He tried throwing himself into his work as an apprentice bathroom installer. He was pretty good at it and under the circumstances, he'd done really well at carving himself a new career in a niche market; installing specialist adaptation equipment in domestic dwellings. The work was lucrative and provided a comfortable standard of living for him and his many girlfriends. You see that was the second thing he'd thrown himself into; lots of meaningless dates which always seemed to end with a blazing row and the family name yet again being tarnished by being dragged through the mire.

His final escapade was the heavy drinking, as Sam lacked the capacity for moderation as he was, what you'd call, an "all or nothing" kind of guy and the drinking was starting to get way out of hand. In fact the family name had continued to be dragged through the mud as Sam found himself being barred from more public houses than he cared to remember. Sam's mum Irene had had enough! She'd allowed him to stay at home in order to keep an eye on him and hoped one day he would see the light and come to his senses.

The final straw for Irene came when she found her son slumped against their conservatory at the back of the house; he was totally inebriated and looked pathetic lying there in his own mess. Something within her broke that night and knew she had to take action. So with the support of her older sister, she sat Sam down the very next day giving him an ultimatum. He either cleaned up his act or he had to leave the family home. Later that day Sam grabbed a few belongings and an overnight bag and without saying a word, left the comfort of his family home, for what he thought would be the last time. Irene felt crushed and had to be restrained by her older sister to prevent her from chasing after her boy.

The proceeding weekend was traumatic for Irene as she just could not stop thinking about her son; what was he up to and what if he was drunk in the gutter somewhere and with that, the tears just continued to flow. For Sam, it was just another rejection to add to the pile and so for him, business as usual; continued bouts of drinking and, should the opportunity arise, some womanising. He spent his first evening on a pal's sofa and the following evening with a complete stranger drinking well into the small hours. Come Sunday the cracks were starting to appear as Sam was starting to miss his home comforts and truth be told, he was starting to feel totally lost and out of his depth. He needed to get a little air and a fresh perspective, in order to clear his head before hooking up with his pals that afternoon in preparation for the big game. There was no need to make excuses to the stranger who lay motionless on the bed next to him, so he made his way out of the dingy flat he was in and headed in search of his trusty steed; his van. After several mobile calls to establish where his van was, he jumped in and headed to a mates' for a quick wash and change of clothes before meeting everyone at The Dog and Trumpet for a few liveners. After more than enough drink to sink a battle cruiser, the lads made their way to the next watering hole which was close to the tube station in south west London. The usual mix of close to the knuckle banter, coupled with copious amounts of beer continued right up until finally reaching the ground.

Although Sam had consumed his fair share of drink, for some reason the mix of booze and banter were having little or no effect on him. Instead he remained quiet and subdued just sitting, staring out of the pub window watching passing traffic and fans being shepherded towards their football cathedral. His silence did not go unnoticed; the lads tried to engage Sam by ruffling his feathers with ridicule and derogatory jokes in order to lift his mood but without realising it, Sam had come to an emotional crossroads and now was the time for him to have a good hard look at his lifestyle. They left the pub and made their way towards the stadium singing the usual offensive, if not slander-ous, chants which soon, sporadically changed hands between the different groups of fans as they neared the entrance to the ground. A final drink in the cordoned-off (caged) areas for good measure and the lads passed through the turnstiles and down towards their regular seats. There was the usual tension in the air as both sets of fans hit full voice shouting abuse or dirty ditties towards one another in the hope of getting a bite by winding someone up. The game soon kicked off and the deafening noise level of the crowd rocketed as the fans cheered for their team and booed their opponents.

Mid way through the 1st half Sam stopped watching the game. He sat back in his seat and looked skyward, the last ebb of light had disappeared behind gray clouds and night was starting to descend. He looked around at his mates, guys he had known for almost a decade and watched their wave of responses as the game peaked and troughed. Their combined, unwavering jeers and shouts of abuse and injustice towards the Ref for not giving a simple throw or free kick in their favour was relentless. He watched as if time stood still as fans in, what appeared to be, slow motion where jumping and throwing their fists in the air either in jubilation or utter condemnation of a poor pass or mistake made by one of their players. He watched his mates and thousands of fans as they bounced up and down in their seats in a rhythmic motion. It looked utterly ridiculous seeing grown men engrossed in this kind of war cry enchantment but you could tell they just loved the camaraderie and the sense of being part of a larger than life cause, which of course was something Sam himself had bought into a long time ago.

Sam stood and then sat back down again. He was perplexed. "What on earth is going on with me?" he wondered. He rocked in his chair and cradled his knees and then held his head in his hands. Tears were starting to form around his eyes and were soon followed by a constant dry sob that kept hitting the back of his throat and before he knew it he was sobbing like a baby. Initially no one could see the state he was in because of all of the commotion going on around but he didn't care either way. He just rocked in his cherished season ticket chair and cried out. He missed his dad so much. He should have been there with him now. He missed playing his beloved football. Yes, he'd been rejected but if truth be told, he'd never really wanted to be a professional footballer in the first place. He was just trying to relive his dad's dream in his own life and that was only going to end one way – in failure! Sam knew in his heart of hearts that all of this had to stop right now; the drinking, the casual encounters with girls and the madcap crazy behaviour with a group of friends that didn't really know each other anyway! Hanging on to past hurts and rejection was weighing him down and making his life a misery fuelled by bitterness, anger and resentment. No more! He needed to take some time out, reflect but then let go of the past and move on with the new. A fresh start for a man who wanted to turn his life around and have significance in his local community. He stood and walked out of the stadium, right there and then. He'd loved his time as a blues fan and knew that he would remain true blue for the rest of his days. But for now, he needed some quiet and tranquillity if he was going to make some significant changes in his life and that would start by heading home and making amends with his mum.

Irene was surprised when she saw her boy on the doorstep and was initially hesitant to open the door fully to welcome him in (as her sister had told her she needed to show some tough love towards Sam). But as soon as she saw his tearstained face and sensed that look of brokenness about him, she knew instinctively that she'd got her boy back. She grabbed him and held him close and they both sobbed in each other's arms. The weeks that followed were used as a great opportunity for mother and son to find their way back to each other. Sam took a couple of weeks off from his work which allowed him to re-charge his batteries and help with some much needed DIY around his home.

One evening, Irene broached the subject about his plans for the future. He was, of course, welcome to stay with her for as long as he wished but she questioned how he felt about his work. Sam turned to her and explained that he actually really enjoyed his work and was happy to continue in his role but maybe venture out alone and start his own company as a builder. He also went on to say how he would love to return to playing football and was considering approaching Handley Park to see if they had any opportunities. He looked to gauge her reaction as he felt really nervous sharing his ambition but his apprehension was short lived and soon cast aside when he saw the look of joy on her face.

"Your dad would be so proud Sam," declared an emotional Irene. "He used to love The Home Guards."
"The Home what?" asked Sam.

She went on to explain how his dad used to love going along to watch his local team; Handley Park. "Their nickname was the home guard, probably after old man Thompson but that's another story. He'd even helped introduce an old army buddy of his to that old miserable so and so, Mike Phillips. You see your dad used to play for Mike years ago; he was part of the squad that was promoted to the football league proper but your dad left soon after as Mike decided to get all high and mighty and seemed to forget the blokes that helped him get there." explained Irene. "Anyway, old misery guts was looking for an assistant coach and your dad introduced him." continued Irene. "Now what was his name?" Big Ron? No, Big Bill, no. What was it? Ah yes, that's it. It was Big Mac. They used to be inseparable, him and your dad back in their old army days. I don't know if he is there anymore, especially after Mike Phillips fell ill, but you never know; you could give him a try." suggested Irene.
Sam stood up, walked over to his mum and kissed her on the forehead. For some reason that name Big Mac meant something about his future. He loved the thought that this man had known his father well and decided there and then that he would search

out this Big Mac. Maybe he could help Sam kick-start his football all over again but at the very least he would love to hear some old stories about his dad.

17

Date Night

The array of street food delivered to their table booth was both pretty impressive and rather excessive as Tony, when in the zone, was more than capable of packing it away when called upon. But tonight, for some reason, he was not in the mood to fill his boots and tuck in to his favourite Empanadas. No, his mind was well and truly focused elsewhere and his wife Helen had had enough.

"Okay time-out. I know I said the subject of football was off limits tonight, but I can't stand it anymore." She continued "Let's have it. Let's have what's on your mind right now."

Tony, slightly off guard, tried to protest insisting that this evening was to be all about them spending some quality time together. However, like all best- laid plans it wasn't to be! You see, Tony just couldn't stop thinking about his recent meeting with Clay.

"I don't get it darling," he commented shaking his head "I just don't get it. As you know, I made a few discreet enquiries concerning Clay and his whereabouts before finally plucking up the courage and boldly knocking on his front door." Continuing he said "The strange thing I just can't seem to get my head round was that he said he'd been expecting me."

Helen, now perplexed, put her drink down and looked at her husband. "But how is that possible?"

"I know," hollered Tony "that's exactly what I thought!"

"Did you ask him how?"

"I did," advised Tony.

"And?" challenged Helen.

"Well, to begin with he started telling me about some vivid dream or other involving Handley Park Rangers and how we were about to embark on something pretty special."

"Wow," declared Helen raising her hands outward. "and what was that something special?"

"I don't know as I suggested that maybe he was getting a little ahead of himself and that I'd only called round to see if he fancied a coffee and a chat."

This time Helen threw her hands upwards in despair "Typical bloke's response trying to rain on someone's parade," goaded Helen.

"I know," rasped Tony rather ashamedly "but later on I did apologise and we did get to have that coffee."

"Good" beamed Helen "and what was the outcome?"

"Well, I'd like to say that I was the one calling the shots but it did not pan out that way."

Helen looked quizzically at her husband but left him to continue.

"Look Helen, he's not like any bloke I know. Possibly, to begin with, I might have had a slight attitude because I allowed my ego to get in the way."

"Possibly?" queried Helen.

"Alright, yes at first I was trying to lay down the law a little and feed him a line about an exciting opportunity I may have coming up with the possible chance of a football trial out."

"And he wasn't taking the bait" affirmed Helen.

"Well, as I said before, I thought he was getting a little ahead of himself." cautioned Tony.

"So? challenged Helen "Did you crash and burn?"

"It certainly looked like it was on the cards. But that all changed when I had this epiphany," smirked Tony.

"Which was?" quizzed Helen.

Hesitantly Tony spat the words out, "Err, that, probably it was me that had gone ahead of himself and not Clay."

Helen laughed. "Would you mind saying that again?"

Disapprovingly he looked across the table at Helen "Don't push it Helen. I'm in unchartered waters here."

She laughed again "I know, that's why I said it."

They sat in silence for a minute before speaking again. "You know, Tony, it seems to me like this guy has really got under your skin. But, in a good way."

"How so?" said Tony.

"Because I think you like him and possibly admire some of his attributes but just won't admit it to yourself." She looked again intently at her husband. "I'm right aren't I?"

Tony coughed nervously and offered a slight frown. "I wouldn't say get under my skin. Maybe more of.....Okay, yes alright he's getting under my skin. I can't explain it really. I just find him fascinating as he seems to have so much depth and I'm not sure whether he even realises it or not."

"Good," exclaimed Helen "maybe you have met your match."

Tony shook his head "No, not even close darling as this guy is streets ahead when it comes to interacting with people. You know sometimes when you think that you're on top of your game and you think you know all there is to know, something like this happens."

"What?" mused Helen.

"You find your humility again and realise none of your ducks are in a row, nothing is pink and fluffy and England aren't going to win the World Cup again."

"All sounds a bit neggie to me," replied Helen.

"Maybe you're right, but knowing this guy exists helps challenge me both personally and professionally to up my game and press on."

Helen looked knowingly at her husband, fluttered her eyes a little "And does this new vigour on life include little ole me?"

Tony laughed out loud "Include you? No, everything starts and finishes with you my darling."

"That's more like it!" Helen laughed. "Now let's tuck in!" And with that the two of them, now engrossed in each other's company, began their Mexican feast.

18

The Hurt Locker - a blokes journey

Graham Krusher was a good, wholesome lad with salt of the earth parents that had nurtured and guided him well over the years. His life had been built on a solid foundation; he was bright, full of spark and mischief and had maintained a disciplined regime of fitness and abstinence from booze and girls throughout his mid to late teenage years. From a young age, he had bought into the ethos his football academy had adopted by acknowledging the fact that raw talent wasn't enough to see you through. What you put in now, - the blood, the sweat and the tears - that's what counted and Graham had certainly ensured that these early years were going to count. And in return, he was highly thought of by his peers at the academy. Expectations were high for his future and, sure enough, within no time at all some of the big boys came knocking with a view to signing this promising young star.

Sadly however, the happy ever after story became shipwrecked somewhere down the line and before long the ugly head of cynicism began to raise its ugly head for poor Graham. And all because of him stopping to try and help a homeless guy. You see, back then Graham was known for wearing his heart on his sleeve and had set out in life with a view to helping out in his local community and working hard to give back a little to his home town. But that all changed after some harmless retail therapy with an old girlfriend late one night whilst shopping in his local town. They were celebrating and out spending money, that hadn't quite arrived in Graham's hands, as he was about to sign a professional football contract with one of the giants of the game. It was deemed that literally overnight he would become a household brand and that his name would be chanted across the terraces for many years to come in what was to him the biggest sport in the world.

He was confident, he was alive, and he was full of life and about to hit the financial big time and probably never want for anything again. But that all changed when he came across a man sitting upright between 4 sets of double doors at the south entrance to the central shopping mall. It was December, all the decks were out and the usual Christmas songs were bellowing through the walkways. To the majority of the Christmas shoppers this chap was invisible but to Graham the site of this sorry looking man was pulling on his heart strings, especially as it was so cold outside and his toes were protruding from worn out trainers. Graham kneeled down to talk with the man. Instinctively he could tell that the man was out of it, but who could blame him given his circumstances and the freezing temperatures he was facing? The only reason he was wedged between the automatic doors was to feel the effect of the heat bellowing from above the doors every time they opened, but he knew his stay there would be short lived as security would soon pass by and move him on. Graham asked him a couple of questions about his plight; ***note by author; interesting isn't it if a chap ever engages with someone who is homeless. They will ask so many challenging and often difficult if not pertinent questions about why and how and when homelessness had come upon them which is often the complete opposite to their normal social etiquette of asking no more than the usual surface questions of; "how you doing?" "I'm fine, how you doing?" "Oh I'm fine" and that's about as deep as the puddle gets.

Anyway, it turns out this homeless chap, Kieran, was from Leicester, he'd split with a long term girlfriend and struggled to cope. He'd managed to persevere for the best part of 6 months before succumbing to an ongoing addiction to drink and drugs and finally losing his flat, his job along with any dignity he had left. The story moved Graham to the point where he later went off and sought out a pair of trainers at his own expense and returned to Kieran where he discreetly handed them over. Although Kieran wasn't completely compos mentis, Graham could tell he was grateful and their brief encounter ended there or so Graham thought. Unbeknown to him, their paths would cross again later when he witnessed someone attempting to steal Kieran's newly acquired trainers whilst he was dozing - during the commotion Kieran had been disturbed and had given chase to the two men who were involved in the theft. This prompted Graham to join the foray by giving chase and as the men reached the local farm produce mini market they all turned to square up to each other in preparation for a scrap. Kieran was, of course, in no position to defend himself or create any form of attack and instead ended up collapsed in a heap on the floor with one of the men standing over him menacingly shouting abuse. As the man prepared to throw one further punch towards Kieran, Graham decided he could no longer stand by and do nothing so he jumped in by hurtling his full body weight upon him. Both men were now trying to weigh the other up as they prepared to engage for a second time and as they entangled, Graham managed to get the upper hand of his assailant by dropping his left shoulder which caused his opponent to lose his balance and crash to the ground. As he turned to defend himself once more, he felt a surge of pain shooting through his left thigh which caused him to stop what he was doing and drop to the floor. As he looked down he realised that his leg was bleeding - probably from a knife wound. The flow of blood was intense and he was starting to feel a little faint so he lay down and elevated his leg and as he looked around he saw his girlfriend crying hysterically, some people rushing towards him whilst others were looking on. Everything seemed to be happening in slow motion. He lay motionless on the polished concrete floor slipping in and out of consciousness and as the lights from his eyes began to fade, he saw on the periphery the silhouette of a man escaping through the growing crowd. It was Kieran hastily retreating amongst the masses sporting none other than a pair of brand new white sneakers.

For Graham the next 12 weeks were no more than a blur. Half his time was spent in hospital before being released under the watchful care of his loving parents. Eventually two weeks later, he commenced a rigorous regime of intensive physiotherapy in order to regain the vital strength needed in his upper thigh if he was to ever have any chance of walking freely without a limp or the aid of a stick. As summer finally peaked, hitting its high temperatures, Graham was discharged from hospital and declared fit and well. Problem was, on the outside yes, he was better and lucky to be, alive but on the inside he was so angry because he knew it would take months if not years for him to build up the necessary muscle strength and fitness level required for him to be even considered match fit. Right now Graham felt like he was out in the wilderness. His dream of a full time career as a professional footballer was down the swanny, as no one right now was prepared to consider signing him; that ship had set sail just after Christmas. His finances were in tatters, his girlfriend had jumped ship in pursuit of another chap destined for the big time and the petty thieves that had created all of the mayhem had never been found or brought to justice along with the elusive Kieran who'd never been seen or heard of again. It was as if that night had been nothing but a bad dream and he felt sure that any day soon he would wake up and all would be well in the garden. That was, of course, until he looked down at the stark reminder on his thigh and felt his way along the 9" Keloid scar that sat so proudly above his quadricep muscle.

Weeks turned into months then into years as Graham tried to make sense of it all. He questioned himself "was I a bad person? Had I wronged someone in a former life?" After all, he'd only tried to help a bloke down on his luck and now misfortune seemed to have made its way to his door and he just did not understand why. He could not sleep and was becoming more and more reliant on antidepressant drugs and sleeping pills to help him through each hazy day and what seemed like an eternal night. He'd even tried counselling and group therapy sessions for victims of crime but had soon quit after no more than two or three sessions. At best, his life was flat-lining as he just could not seem to cope with it all anymore; everything around him seemed grey in colour and pointless. Yes, that's it; pointless and mean-ingless. This life he was living right now was not the life he had chosen or signed up for. No, it was a sham. He was supposed to be out on the field of dreams being worshipped and idolised by his adoring fans!

Graham was on the brink of chucking in the towel and ending it all. He'd even hatched a plan of how and where he would do away with himself. But truth be told, when push came to shove the very thought grieved his soul. However, before long he finally hit rock bottom and felt like there was nothing else left for him. His parents were away camping, not that they wanted to as they were so worried about their boy, but they desperately needed a change of scenery to help give them a little clarity about things. Without a thought for anyone else or the consequences of his actions, Graham carelessly hit the bottle hard and after an epic binge drinking raid of his parents' drinks cabinet complete with a cocktail of prescription pills, he passed out, but thankfully was found by a friendly neighbour who'd been out walking her dog in a local park. She stumbled across him slumped on a park bench, completely inebriated. As she knew of his plight, she had quickly raised the alarm and he was soon taken to a local hospital for treatment where he spent the next three nights on a drip before being referred yet again for counselling. But this time it was mandatory.

It was during these sessions that Graham's life began to take a turn for the better. He finally had his chance to re-live the events that had caused him such pain, anguish and regret. Instead of the constant flashbacks that had been attacking his mind for the last two years, he had a chance to offload his pain in a safe environment and without judgement or someone trying to fix him up. He felt freer than he had at any stage in his life and it was all thanks to the team of counsellors that had supported him and invested in him but also to one crazy, off the charts ex-prison chaplain otherwise known as "The Running Man".

*** Footnote; author's thoughts about how men usually respond to questions about self. ***

19

The Running Man

Mark Dellany Smith had been around the block more times than he cared to remember in his fleeting 55 years here on the earth. He seemed to have cornered the market when it came to the virtue of being street wise amongst the revellers in the school of hard knocks. By rights, he should have been out for the count on more than several occasions during his tenure as a teenage boy, youth and finally a man but the memo never reached his shores and his refusal to allow life to get the better of him remained intact along with his refusal to conform or quit. This battle-scarred-life led him to his life's vocation of not quitting on others. He refused to quit on the school kid that was different and didn't seem to fit in. Or the homeless chap that appeared invisible to most. Or the single parent mum trying to make ends meet whilst keeping her boys off the streets of a night. Or the off the rails teenager intent on constantly hitting the self destruct button or the young offender that couldn't find an opportunity for work as everyone had written him off.

You see Mark seemed to thrive and come alive when he saw a

need in another and loved to step in, roll his sleeves up and get his hands dirty. This was especially true for all of those who had fallen to the wayside and had no hope, which is exactly where he came across an angry young Graham Krusher, whose life had gone completely out of control and for what? Helping a homeless guy. He could tell this young man was stuck and suffering with deep emotional turmoil. It was as if he had a civil war raging from within his very being and had no idea how to get out of this prison and so Mark did what he does best; he closed the hole just below his nose and listened and listened and listened until the lad just ran out of things to say. In fact, Graham was beginning to think Mark was mute until finally, one day, after a particularly trying session, he told Graham how he liked to run. I believe Graham was hoping for a little more in the way of input but that is all he received at that moment in time. Nothing more but it was enough to keep him interested and want to know more about this larger than life character.

Even after Graham had finished his counselling sessions, he continued to meet up with Mark in what would become a fruitful relationship that would take Graham from the brink into a new life that was full of so much hope and promise. After months of friendly banter, Graham finally acquiesced and joined Mark for an evening run. Initially the pace was easy and the distance no more than a mile or so, but steadily Mark turned the screw on Graham as he gradually upped the pace and extended the length of run by changing the route or scenery.

They would often stop, sit and talk somewhere remote before continuing on but this evening, given the warm temperatures with light breeze, they just sat. Graham asked Mark how he had found his interest in running to which Mark went on to share the short story of a man who'd inspired him many years ago. He spoke of a tenacious Australian man by the name of Cliff Young. To all intents and purposes he was no more than a farm labourer who had dedicated his life to the family business. Money was scarce; in fact money was so tight that the family were unable to provide horses, dogs or tractors to help tend the farm or keep the sheep in check. Instead Cliff covered the 2000 acre farm by running across it, especially if the sheep needed rounding up during a storm. Many years later, at the age of 61, (Mark gave Graham a quick sideway glance to make sure he wasn't about to poke fun at his age) Cliff entered himself into a long distance 500 mile foot race going from Sydney to Melbourne. Initially he was refused entry, as he appeared to have little or no experience in this form of competition and to the organisers a chap wearing overalls and work boots did not bode well. Finally Cliff was given an opportunity and as expected once the race got underway, the 150 world class athletes disappeared beyond the horizon. Unperturbed, Cliff continued along his merry way running at a steady pace not only during the day but also all through the night (Cliff had no idea all contestants were supposed to rest of a night) until by the fifth day, he had caught them all and won the race.

Soon after, Cliff Young became a national hero and rightly so but what really spoke to Mark, was his underdog status and his ability to endure and keep going no matter what the circumstances. Mark's short story had the desired effect on Graham which allowed, over a gradual period of time, the opportunity for Mark to push Graham further and further to his physical and spiritual limits until the time came for Mark to broach the subject of a return to the game of football.

"Why not?" challenged Mark whilst double knotting the laces of his trainers.

"No Mark, leave it, just don't go there!" implored Graham.

"Go where?" coaxed Mark.

Graham gave him a scathing look. "You know where."

"No, you tell me" goaded Mark.

"I can't," croaked Graham. "You know I can't."

"That's not true," declared Mark. "I know you can."

A silence descended between them both; Mark recognised it straightaway and knew what to do (remain silent) whilst Graham felt truly uncomfortable and was about to flee the conversation. Mark was willing the lad on in his head; come on Graham you can do it.

The silence continued for what felt like an eternity before Graham could stand it no more and blurted out

"Okay, okay I miss playing. I miss the camaraderie of the team. I miss the petrichor scent of the turf. I'm lost, you know I am."

"No you're not. You know, for the first time you have been honest with yourself and that in itself is liberating," affirmed Mark. "You can do this son. You can. I believe in you."

Graham stood cradling his head with both arms. He turned his back on Mark and looked down at the scar on his thigh. "Look at it Mark, look at it."

"I know" sighed Mark, "but your strength is back fully and you are ready. To what degree is up to you and the way you approach your future, either as a victim or a victor, is your choice. So what is it to be?"

It was the first time Mark had played hardball with Graham in their friendship and he felt the time was right.

"So where do I start, clever clogs?" challenged Graham.

"Now it's funny you should say that as I know just the man" declared Mark. "He'll soon whip you into shape".

Graham looked at Mark. He never ceased to amaze Graham with the amount of people he knew and for the first time in years he began to feel a bit happier about the future.

20

The trail to glory begins (well sort of)

Rumour had it that a late Indian summer was destined for the blue flag shores of a rather bruised and battered post Brexit-Blighty. The England squad, with its wealth of talent, yet again proved an utter disappointment on the big stage at the European finals, exiting early from the tournament. But for the good old folk of Handley Park, it was business as usual with their bustling high street market and canal festival which extended along the towpath of the Grand Union, leading into the main park and playing fields located at the foot of the town.

As for Handley Park Rangers, the Extra Preliminary round of the FA Cup that beckoned proved a pretty haphazard affair. The exciting home tie was scheduled for the 1st weekend in August but on the day, it proved very lacklustre with both teams playing well below par. With 10 minutes of "painful to watch" play left, it was more than obvious that both teams had decided to "live to fight another day" and play-out for a draw. With the game now running at a snail's pace, an anticipated nil-nil result was expected had it not been for a misjudged pass back by the visitors' defence to their rather bored keeper. In the twinkling of an eye, Handley Park's lone striker, awoke from his reverie and was on the ball, round the helpless "have-had-nothing- to- do-all game" goalie and soon found himself, at a gentle pace, walking the ball into an empty net. Of course he milked the celebrations, as he turned to greet his teammates and the handful of adoring fans to celebrate. And with that, Handley Park Rangers found themselves through to the next round ready to meet new opponents.

Coupled with this success, the boys even managed to finish their previous season by remaining in the league, having spent best part of it hovering just above the league trap-door. In fairness, it was more luck than judgement as the two teams below them decided to capitulate early on and resigned themselves to life in the lower leagues. The appointment of Tony Jeffs as interim manager was no more than a low-key affair, which suited Nigel down to the ground. His plan to install an unknown body at the helm had come to fruition All he had wanted to do was appease any prying eyes, whilst continuing in the background to plot and scheme in the boardroom playground for a lucrative, quick sale of the club he so despised.

Tony's arrival initially seemed to have little or no effect, as there was no expectation from just about everyone involved, including the dwindling fan base, the players and backroom staff along with the loyal volunteers that helped run the club. This suited Tony as it gave him the opportunity to have a good look around and focus on where he could channel his energy and time. First up was building a relationship with the existing assistant coach, Big Mac, who had worked under the previous manager Mike Phillips for a number of seasons. Tony wanted him on-side, so set about sitting down with him and establishing just where he was at right now with regard to his future at the club. Tony soon noticed just how disillusioned Mac was with everything going on at the club and sensed he looked pretty close to throwing in the towel and quitting. But after spending a good few days with him, listening to many of the problems and issues he had had to face, he realised that Mac genuinely still loved the club and for him that was more than enough to get things going and to hatch a plan of action. So Tony made it his priority to befriend Big Mac and allow him within his circle of trust by opening himself up and giving Mac the chance to see what kind of character he would be working with. That would then let him make his own judgement call as to whether they had a future together.

As for Mac, yes, he was very coy initially and tried his best not to be cynical towards a man he barely knew and to all intents and purposes had about as much knowledge of the game of football as Nigel, but over the weeks ahead he soon realised that Tony definitely had a way about him, he couldn't quite put his finger on it but he liked him and trusted him and for Mac that would do right now. Both Tony and Mac had much in common, including the love of football, and coupled with the many attributes they possessed could, given time, work well together and form a lasting partnership. With this in mind, they set about strategically looking at how they could rebuild their squad which, of course, would be no mean feat considering they had no financial budget at their disposal to attract any up-and-coming talent.

Tony looked to Mac, stopped short for a second with what he was about to say and then just said it anyway;

"Mac, I know you're not a big fan of Darren or his thug of a sidekick Frank and that we have had to make do with keeping things running just to get through the tail end of last season, but

I have to be honest; my gut says these two have to go if we are to see any kind of improvement in form, or morale for that matter, and ideally before the new season kicks in properly."

Mac replied "You know Tony, I could not wish for more than to see the back of those two hoodlums from this club but as you can see, we have no way of replacing them,"

Tony cut in "But I do have a possibility. I've not approached him yet. He's American or well at least I think he is. He used to be a high school first choice quarterback but lives in the UK now after his folks returned."

" Hold on a second," exclaimed Mac, "you want to employ (I'll use that word loosely as you have to pay someone if they are employed) an American quarterback to keep goal for Handley Park Rangers? Are you out of your mind?"

"Well as I said," continued Tony, "I'm not sure he's American but I have watched him play."

"Play! Play where?" challenged Mac.

"Oh, I watched him in goal recently against some of my work colleagues in a local power league game," advised Tony.

"Hold on a minute," gawped Mac "he plays for a local power league team?"

"Well, as I understand it, he was more of a stand in as their regular keeper was ill" noted Tony.

Big Mac threw his hands in the air in dismay. They both remained silent for a time before Tony declared;

"Look Mac. I know you know football inside and out, I get that. But I know people and I'm telling you now this kid is worth a look, trust me!"

Big Mac rubbed the stubble on his chin and slowly nodded his head before saying;

"But you said you'd done no more than grab a coffee with him."

"I know," agreed Tony, "but if you like him then I'll get him, don't worry about that."

"How are you so sure, considering we have no money and very little prospects to entice him here?" observed Mac.

"Just leave that with me," suggested Tony and with that the two men headed out onto the training ground for an early evening session and as they made their way around the pitch towards the gate in the perimeter fence a voice called out:

"Mr. McGrath could I have a word please?" and as the two men turned they faced a rather nervous looking young man.

"You don't know me Mr. McGrath but I believe you knew my father, well my late father – Pete Ryan" declared Sam now looking intently at Big Mac.

"Number 10 shirt," exclaimed Mac instinctively. "We went way back beyond Civvy Street. He was a good man your dad. How's your mum?"

"Oh she is doing just fine thanks Mr. McGrath," beamed Sam.

"It's Mac or Big Mac, okay?" advised Mac.

"Okay," responded Sam.

"So what brings you here son?"

"You Big Mac!" said Sam.

"Me?" said Mac "What do you want from me?"

Sam was caught off guard this time as he wasn't expecting that question yet. "Well.... er, I was just wondering..." babbled Sam.

"Come on, spit it out then lad" snapped Mac.

"Well I'm looking to take up football again and mum mentioned your name" stuttered Sam.

"This ain't no playground to pass the time away!" provoked Mac.

"I know, I know I'm just a little nervous as this is a big deal for me," gulped Sam.

"What's your name son?" demanded Mac.

"It's Sam" squeaked Sam.

"Well, this chap here is Tony Jeffs, the coach of Handley Park

Rangers," stated Mac "and if it is okay with him, I'd like to take a look at what you are made of. So bring your boots here tomorrow night okay?" urged Mac.

"Fine by me," added Tony. "See you tomorrow," and with that the two men turned, continuing their conversation from before.

"Look Tony, just coming back to the dynamic duo for a minute. I have an old friend who's an ex prison chaplain and fitness fanatic. It's just an idea, but why don't we get him involved in this war of attrition and let him put them through their paces? My guess is they will either leave of their own free will or you never know, they may just step up to the plate," advised Big Mac.

"That's not a bad idea Mac, what's his name?" enquired Tony.

"Mark Dellany Smith otherwise known as The Running Man," confirmed Mac.

"Okay I'd like to meet him, he may even be a good addition for the team. Can you set up a meeting with the three of us?" enquired Tony. "But either way Darren is finished in goal. Is that fair enough?"

"That is fine with me," agreed Mac. "Let's just hope your American will be up for it."

"Yeah, let's hope so" quipped Tony.

Sam was buzzed and couldn't wait to share his news with his mum, so hurried back to his van with thoughts racing through his head about how he should play; should he hold back or go all out for it? Then for a split second, he allowed his long term companion, namely fear, the opportunity to fill him with worry about playing football again. What if he didn't cut the mustard? What if he got injured again or was rejected again? But this time, he chose to chase those thoughts from his mind as he pictured his dad with Big Mac in battledress. He could do this. He just needed to believe in himself a bit more.

"Who was Pete Ryan" quizzed Tony.

"Oh he was an old army buddy, we went through quite a bit together back in the day," replied Mac.

"And the lad – what if he doesn't cut it?" queried Tony.

"Then he doesn't make it," stated Mac.

"As easy as that?" asked Tony.

But Mac did not respond as he was thinking of his old comrade and their days together in their elite regiment. They had been through some scrapes together, including some near fatal misses but thanks to Pete they had made it through unscathed. "So that was his boy?" he thought to himself. "Well, if he is anything like his old fella, he'll do just fine," he said under his breath and with that his focus, turned to the players before him "Huddle in guys – let's get going."

21

The motivator, the tactician and the running man start to gel.

The first time they all met was in a quaint country pub just off the roundabout of a main A-road. The pub was very olde worlde with" duck or grouse" low ceilings, complete with rustic beams and a nook with a roaring open fireplace. The Pub food was good and the ale reasonably priced but the chaps were not here to discuss culinary cuisine or the average price of a pint. No, they were here initially for two reasons. One was for Tony to meet Mark and secondly to see if there was any chemistry between the three of them that could ignite a fire of hope within this fledgling football club.

After initial pleasantries, the three of them got down to business, namely; who are you Mark, what are you all about and are you up for the challenge? Tony instinctively knew within the first 5 minutes that this ex-prison chaplain would make an invaluable asset to this team. Tony, as head coach, was the born leader and motivator whilst Big Mac, as assistant manager, was the tactician extraordinaire and Mark? Well, originally he was to offer the team his duties as club chaplain but almost immediately Tony's view changed as he believed that he had so much more to offer. As well as the duty of pastoral care, it became more than apparent that he could fill the role of fitness coach, especially as he was affectionately known as 'The Running Man.' He may well have been a little bit past his sell-by-date but boy, was this guy fit! He would think nothing of going for a 20 mile hike across rough terrain and treat it as no more than a warm up.

As the evening progressed, Tony enquired from both Big Mac and Mark
"How did you guys first meet"?
And for a split second Tony noticed hesitancy in both their demeanours. "What's that all about?" he thought to himself, "probably something to do with Big Mac's days as a soldier in the Special Forces."
But what followed as a discussion was a complete surprise to him. You see Big Mac and Mark first met during a semi final FA cup game back in the late 80's. Both men had separately remained loyal to the reds from a young age and had grown up on all of the pomp and ceremony of the majestic FA Cup. But not only that, they were still enthralled by the excitement and buzz that this long established competition had to offer. They both loved the build up preliminary rounds followed by qualifying matches then finally the introduction of the big guns (which was where their team joined the fun) as small local clubs would fight it out for the chance to face one of the top flight teams, hoping to slay one of the giants of the game by knocking them out of the tournament. Now that was the stuff of legends and both men couldn't get enough of it.
That was until their chance meeting when they were seated next

to each other in the West Stand just above the Leppings Lane terrace. And as both men began to share their stories Tony could see etched on their faces the memory of relived shock and horror playing out in their minds.

 Initially everything was as it should have been with both men eating more than their fair share of Pukka pies and pasties along with drinking copious amounts of lukewarm Bovril. They had both made an effort by creeping out of their comfort zones and acknowledging each other prior to kick off, rather than the usual back turning and aloofness. But what really got them talking was the way in which the terraces below surged in numbers from no more than a few hundred in the build up to kick off to a swelling ocean of bodies that seemed to be swirling around at the mercy of the elements. Both men sensed something was not quite right and soon knew that help was required, as calls for assistance could be heard from below them, along with the first signs of panic beginning to show on many of the faces, as people could no longer move their arms, legs or shoulders. Instinctively Big Mac's training kicked in as he moved forward and lent over the ledge of the stand and began grabbing at arms or legs in order to wrestle people out of their plight to safety. Mark watched Big Mac jumping to it and stood up to join in and help but not before taking a good look around in order to see what help and support was on hand. However, the scene unfolding before his very eyes was worrying to say the least and so Mark made his way to the railings at the very edge of the stand to join Big Mac and began to assist with what was now becoming an emergency. The actual game had commenced play but lasted no more than a few minutes as an eruption of panic had taken hold behind the goal. People were rushing across to assist those trapped against the fences and with that, a crowd was beginning to overflow on to the pitch.

Both men stopped for a minute, pensive in thought and instinctively commenced a ritual of rinsing their hands before clasping them together and looking on with glazed eyes, transfixed on nothing in particular. Instinctively, they both wiped underneath their eyes with the back of their hands and looked up, at once catching each other's eye with a knowing look. They all knew how this story panned out and were in no hurry to take their minds back and relive those harrowing scenes, so instead they opted to sit in silence for what seemed like an age, deep in their own thoughts. Tony had his own memories of that fateful day but chose not to share as he thought the timing was inappropriate. He sensed the pain that both men were feeling from such a tragic experience. It was as if time had stood still for them both, they were stuck and struggling to move on.

Whilst sitting there, thoughts raced through Tony's mind of a time sitting in an intensive care unit in Paddington, London watching his seriously ill father, surrounded by breathing apparatus, slowly doodling with a cheap throwaway pen on a hospital notepad. For some reason, his dad kept writing down telephone number after telephone number from his past. 01 459, no 01 421 06, no 01 the numbers just kept meandering aimlessly across the page. His dad's style of calligraphy although basic, had always been very impressive to Tony but this senseless list of work and home numbers, many of which Tony recognised, was driving him nuts. Maybe it was the affects of the heavy dosage drugs, he wasn't sure, but for some reason it was really upsetting. You see Tony was desperate but unable to communicate with him and he wanted to, no, needed to share so much about the goings on of his father's business and home life. He wanted him to know that he had his back and was doing all he could to shield his father from all of the lies and deceit he had spun for so many years. It was just so frustrating, there he was right in front of him and yet he may as well have been on Mars for all it mattered, as he could not let him know not to worry and just to concentrate on getting better.

As Tony had looked around in frustration, he happened upon a portable Combi TV on the window sill. A football game was on but there seemed to be some sort of problem behind one of the goals. Tony looked pensively at the screen watching the most shocking images he had ever seen beaming back at him of a disaster unfolding at a football ground in Yorkshire.

"I'll never forget it, never!" declared Tony out loud to no one in particular.

"Forget what?" enquired Mac.

"Oh nothing," went on Tony. "It will keep."

All three men were now deeply lost in thought as no words were available to describe how they were feeling right now. So Tony stood, grabbing the guy's glasses. "Let's have another" was all he said and turned to head off to the bar, but in doing so he forgot to duck and felt the full grouse (force) of a 19th century oak beam across his temple. His body flinched in pain and the old fashioned beer jugs clinked together between his hands. Tony composed himself and stood tall, probably to compensate for his rather bruised ego and as he looked back he found both Big Mac and Mark holding their sides and crying with laughter whilst at the same time trying to hide their response. He tried to offer up his best Paddington Bear stare (the most stern look he had) which made the guys cry with laughter even more until eventually, all Tony could do was join them and soon began laughing uncontrollably at his own misfortune. The barman, who'd watched the whole thing, told Tony that he would bring their drinks over whilst reminding him to watch his step as he headed back to his table which produced even more laughter from his table. He sat down with the guys. He looked at Mark and said "Look, I know it's very spontaneous, but let's make a toast Mark, I would like you to be a new member of our management team."

In response, Mark looked a little surprised, but showed no signs of disinterest so Tony continued.

"There'll be no pay, or recognition for that matter, but I'd love to welcome you aboard to our ever so slightly battered and bruised ship. She may not look much, but she's yours if you will have her."

For a brief moment silence ensued before Mark responded,

"How could I refuse such an auspicious opportunity, I accept wholeheartedly!"

And with that, they clinked glasses and each took a swig of ale.

"Now down to business," began Tony "we have a lot to discuss. The way I see it, the club has little or no financial resources. The current owner has very little interest in the club or its future and from what I can gather nobody is being paid. Have I missed anything?"

"No, that just about covers everything," confirmed Mac.

"Sounds so enticing, what's not to love?" laughed Mark.

"Well, if I'm being honest, that is exactly why I'm so drawn to this challenge. It kind of reminds me of a young Ernest Shackleton and his quest to explore the Antarctic. Minus the snow of course," said Tony.

"I could do with a bit of that right now. You know, looking for everyday men who were up for a huge challenge, completely out of their depth and with no regard for personal gain or reward," beamed Tony. "I love the story about Shackleton's alleged newspaper advert in the swinging twenties. He spoke about men being wanted for his endurance expedition with the following caption: 'Men wanted for hazardous journey. Low wages, bitter cold, long hours of complete darkness. Safe return doubtful! Honour and recognition in event of success!' Pretty impressive stuff don't you think? Now that is the kind of goal and objective I want our players to yearn and strive for. What do you think?"

"Well I was beginning to think you were a little off the charts so your thoughts do no more than corroborate that. I have to say my time at the club thus far has been utterly disappointing, so for me I'd rather go out in a blaze of glory than fizzle out in the Shires. So I'm in!" announced Big Mac.

"And there is no going back for me either," exclaimed Mark, "sounds far too interesting for me to miss out on. I'm in!" confirmed Mark.

"Right then let's have a good look at who we currently have on the books and decide if we need to cull certain characters who will not buy into our ethos and look to recruit some lads who are up for the challenge ahead," said Tony.

And with that, the guys spent the next couple of hours discussing the club, the players and Nigel's lack of interest along with any possible new recruits.

"What an excellent start," expressed Tony.

"Now that is music to my ears," said Big Mac. "In fact, let's toast to the end of an era for Handley Park Rangers, of being downtrodden and put upon by the likes of Mike Phillips and let's celebrate new beginnings."

"I can see this being a long, long night" cautioned Tony as both he and Mark raised their glasses for what, certainly, wouldn't be the last time of the evening.

22

Frank Malone - The Volcano

Frank's love of football began at the tender age of 4. His dad had rushed home excitedly from work one sunny August evening. He had woken Frank up out of bed (much to the annoyance of his mum) and soon had him downstairs in the back garden, setting up their brand new portable goal ready for a kick about. From that moment on, Frank was hooked- especially as it allowed him to hang out with his dad. A few years later, Frank's dad signed him up with a local youth team and would religiously take Frank along, where he would often stay to watch his boy as well as offer some encouraging words of wisdom. But that would all change when, completely out of the blue, his hero of a dad (the man he loved beyond compare) left the family home to start a new life with another woman. For Frank it was the end of his world. He was eleven years of age and totally lost without the one man he loved and trusted completely. At such a tender age Frank was all at sea, totally lost and had no idea why his dad had rejected him. His mum, once known as a bubbly, larger than life character, just wasn't available to Frank right now as she was so overcome with her own grief and pain and rejection and would often be found, at home, by Frank, huddled on the sofa in a drunken stupor staring into nothingness.

The only saving grace in Frank's life, that offered him some form of solitude and stability, was his football. It allowed him to forget, if only momentarily, the rather painful, turbulent theme of dysfunction that was running right through the centre of his family life. He continued to play his football as his mum managed to shake herself down and take her boy, if only for a short period of time, as the drop offs and pickups became rather sporadic until eventually fizzling out altogether. Frank, now pretty much left to his own devices, managed to make his own way there. He was tired of being let down at the last minute and for some reason felt more in control of his own life when his family weren't around to let him down.

A couple of months later Frank hooked up with a new player; they had lots in common, and soon become best buds, hanging out most evenings at his mates house, if anything just to avoid the turbulence at home. After a while, the lads become inseparable. They journeyed to school together and went to football training and matches, thanks to his mate's dad who would pick them up and chauffeur them around, pretty much, to every game. Well, that was until one evening on the way back from an away game, the dad decided to drop his son off first as he had some homework to finish. The dad made Frank sit in the front and asked lots of questions about his football, school life and then finally how things were going at home. The dad explained that you didn't need to be a genius to realise that Frank's home life was tough.

Frank was vulnerable and felt uncomfortable talking about home, but the dad was a good listener and so Frank relaxed and opened up. The dad said he had to stop for a minute to pick something up at his workplace. He asked Frank to help him carry a parcel out to the car which Frank happily agreed to, but things turned a little uncomfortable in the dad's small office when he made an inappropriate move on Frank and tried to get physical with him in the wrong sense of the word. Frank was totally shocked and ran from the room, out to the car park and into the night. It took him some time to find his bearings but he managed to find his way home. It would be great to say that Frank was able to talk to someone, perhaps his mum or absent dad but he had no one to share his fear, shame or disgust with. For a time he made excuses and skipped training, along with matches, and before long he'd dropped out of the team all together. His school work took a nosedive and he became more and more insular as the weeks passed. His mate called for a time but eventually gave up. As for his mum, she just raised her hands in despair as this boy of hers had become unrecognizable and she was no longer able to handle or keep him under control.

Eventually Frank's trail of destruction led him to make a bold statement by fighting with a well known bully whilst in the school playground and to his pleasure, came out on top. And from that moment on, Frank let his fists do the talking and never allowed anyone or anything to get close to him. Funny enough, Frank did return to football playing for a Saturday team before eventually joining Handley Park Rangers but this time there was no grace or fancy footwork to his playing style. Now, tactically speaking, it was straightforward as Frank was far more interested in taking out the man rather than obtaining the ball. In fact, Frank's view was if he managed to reach the ball well, that was just a bonus! Every time he saw a player in his way he was keen to inflict some sort of physical pain because, when he pulled on a football jersey, all he saw standing in front of him was that scumbag of a dad.

Mike Phillips originally signed Frank purely as he thought he looked and acted like a thug so he might add some aggression in defence. Plus he thought it might help his son, Darren, as he seemed better equipped at letting in goals rather than saving any. Big Mac protested as he could tell straightaway that the lad had issues with authority and lacked any form of self discipline but as usual Mike waved Mac away, ignoring any advice as, of course, he knew best.

After Mike's exit from the club, Frank continued to live up to his namesake (namely the volcano) by brawling and trying to break the record for the number of yellow and red cards awarded until the arrival of Tony, who miraculously managed to steady the ship. But it was the presence of the funny looking running man that spelled change for Frank. Not on his part, no, as Frank had his head down and was driving forward trying to inflict a whole lot of pain. No, it was Mark. You see, somehow he was able to see right through Frank's out of control behaviour and he wasn't buying it. In fact, his very presence unnerved Frank to the point where he would keep his distance from him, hoping to not engage. But sooner or later he just knew that this little bloke had his number pegged and that their paths would cross in the not so distant future.

23

The terrible twosome on the ropes

With three new signings under their belt and the option for a fourth within the coming weeks, things were starting to look up for Handley Park Rangers. There was a buzz about the place coupled with a fresh scent of optimism on the horizon. For once the management team at the helm seemed to be working in unison and were actually keen to be there. Sam Ryan, Graham Krusher and Clay Jackson had all completed a trial and had each performed well on the day. Yes, there were signs of nerves and their fitness levels required work but the management team were in no doubt that these lads would be an asset to the club, especially as it appeared that the three of them seemed to bond really well together. As for Darren Phillips and Frank Malone, both guys had been given the option by Big Mac of leaving the club forthwith or spending the next couple of months under the care and watchful eye of Mark. They both, of course, ranted and raved about the decision and threatened to walk, stating that a number of clubs had expressed an interest in them (which of course they hadn't). Finally they acquiesced and agreed to spend a total of 60 days away from Handley Park, initially focusing on fitness levels before delving into some form of much needed anger management evaluation.

In the first week both men fell into the trap of underestimating not only Mark's ability as a trainer but also Mark as a man. In fact, they spent best part of the first day driving their banter bus with the express aim of character assassinating him, hoping that he would either take the bait and bite back or give up his futile attempts of rehabilitation. But little did they know that the man before them had spent the best part of two decades helping mentor and counsel category A inmates who were serving at the pleasure of Her Majesty. Mark was quite happy for these troubled men to ridicule and joust their way through the first day, as cometh the morning they would commence a leisurely jog across the moors before competing, after their day jobs, in one of Mark's makeshift assault courses - which normally included the use of lots of old agricultural tyres. Initially both Darren and Frank found the run no more than a little tiresome, especially it being 06.00am, but as they passed the half hour stage and headed towards the 45 minute mark they started to labour a little - which just so happened to be the time that Mark was just getting warmed up. Some 5 miles out of town there sits a crossroads with a war memorial set back from the road where "Old man Thompson" kept his famous allotments that helped keep the town nourished during wartime. This was to be the marker for the half way stage, which was when they would commence the journey back home. But what they did not realise was that this was where Mark would up the tempo and start pushing the lads a little harder, before stretching them further still, with a blistering pace that, to all intents and purposes, could not be maintained. All with the express aim of breaking down these aggressive, counter- productive negative behaviour patterns that these two youths had come to rely on for such a long time.

Just over a mile from home, first Darren, closely followed by Frank collapsed in a heap along the country lane that led past the petrol station and into the church square. Darren couldn't speak and was coughing and spluttering all over the place whereas Frank, on the other hand, couldn't even mutter a sound or clench a fist which was exactly where Mark wanted them right now, knowing that come the evening, when they would start cardio training, their complaining would return with intensity. Mark stopped running and turned back to the men to show a little concern and empathy.

"How we doing guys?" Mark asked compassionately.

No response was forthcoming from the two men lying in the overgrown grass by the side of the road so Mark sat down next to them and waited patiently. Eventually Darren sat up closely followed by Frank. They were not impressed with having to endure this whimsical attempt at having them fall into line with the new regime however, both men, although slightly out of salts, remained defiant in their quest to rebel and fight the system. The three of them finally got back into stride and made their way back home all agreeing to meet that evening at the knolls. The assault course Mark had laid out for the guys was tough and like earlier in the day both men soon found themselves up against it and struggling for breath but both persevered and finished within a reasonable time. Afterwards on their way home, the pair of them spoke about hatching a plan to take Mark out of the equation. Who did this old preacher guy think he was trying to outrun us and out muscle us with his pathetic excuse for an assault course? So the very next day and with real fervent intent I might add, the lads met with Mark, at the agreed time and place to commence warm up stretches before jogging. But this time, Darren and Frank arranged for a little surprise for their preacher friend. A mate of theirs happened to be out on the Moors walking his dog, which somehow managed to jump loose of its lead and run off in the direction of the early morning runners. This rather zealous Doberman Pinscher had a bit of a reputation for attacking any passerby that moved at speed, therefore any unsuspecting jogger was fair game. As the three of them left town heading up to the Moors, Mark sensed that all was not as it should be as his two cohorts seemed far too eager, especially after yesterday's whining and groaning. And sure enough, Mark's intuition was spot on as in the distance he noticed a four legged foe (not friend) moving at quite a pace towards them. Only thing is it wasn't them anymore, for when he turned round both Darren and Frank were nowhere to be seen. At the last thicket, the men had crossed a cattle grid and jumped a flint wall, knowing full well that any minute now a foaming-at-the-mouth canine would arrive with only one thing on his mind; lunch!

Both men were laughing, expecting to see "the running man" running for his life back down the hill towards town but instead, after the initial commotion of the dog barking and growling prior to launching an attack, all they heard was silence. Darren and Frank looked at each other puzzled before braving it and peering above the wall, thinking that maybe the dog had killed Mark. Panicking, they stood up in unison and looked along the wall not sure now what they would expect to find. Maybe the blood splattered corpse of the old preacher? But instead all they found was Mark with his hand gently stroking the head of this now placid, rather obedient Doberman sitting at Mark's side. Both men were speechless when Mark finally looked over and commented

"Are we done with the shenanigans yet or are we going to continue with the play acting as I'm rather keen to get back to the job in hand."

Darren and Frank fumbled their way over the wall both grazing legs and falling to the floor as the morning dew on the flint made for a slippery surface. They stood up slightly dishevelled and looking rather sheepish, unable to look Mark in the eyes.

"Well?" said Mark.

"How did you know?" asked Darren finally.

"Because that's what troubled lads do when they are bored or up against it; they dig themselves a hole," said Mark.

Frank then piped up "What about the dog?"

"Oh that's easy," said Mark. "If I can make a dog more scared of me than I of him, then it's no contest."

The dog incident subdued the mood of both Darren and Frank as they soon realised there was more to this preacher bloke than met the eye and so the next couple of weeks soon passed by without incident. Well, that is not strictly true. You see, Mark organised a little welcoming committee of his own for the boys towards the end of the second week. It was their usual 06.00am kick off with warm ups before jogging up onto the moors. But this time, as they reached the old war memorial, the lads were slightly ahead, which made a bit of a change, and left them feeling pretty pleased with themselves. Their progress to date had been a little slow but there was a sense that the lads were starting to take things more seriously, which was why the old man had not been on their case much this week. Plus, surprisingly, he seemed to be labouring a little and was behind. In fact, as they turned to check his progress they became concerned as he was nowhere to be seen. They looked around, scanning the horizon concerned just in case he'd collapsed in a heap somewhere, but instead all they spotted was a Doberman Pinscher moving at a fair rate of knots in their direction. Both lads panicked, inadvertently stumbling into each other before running aimlessly hoping to find somewhere to hide, but no flint wall was at hand to save them this time, so the boys did what they do best; they pegged it and ran full speed back towards town closely followed by a rather hungry Doberman.

As they reached the bottom of the moors, they happened upon Mark, sitting comfortably on a wall admiring the sun breaking through the clouds and illuminating a wonderful rock formation that sat proud of a small stream just below. He had his legs crossed and was drinking a freshly ground coffee purchased from Giovanni's cafe in town. He waved an arm casually at the lads as they flew past him at neck breaking speed.

"How we doing today lads? Just admiring the view, isn't it a marvellous day?" was all he said as they sped past him. "I guess I'll see you later then!" which kind of fell on deaf ears as the lads disappeared out of sight. Mark eventually stood up and smiled at the same time muttering to himself

"I think we're starting to get somewhere now."

Gradually, he made his way down the hill in the direction of Darren and Frank, knowing that as funny this little episode was, this was the "in" he had been looking for to engage with them both and begin their journey of restoration. Of course, the next few weeks were no picnic for any of them as, after all, these were two very troubled kids but gradually as a new month dawned, the three of them commenced an anger management process that Mark had used many times whilst working with inmates in prison. A couple of weeks in, it became more than apparent that these two lads before him were actually decent boys that had been labelled, by society, as rotten eggs and it was all because they carried deep father wounds. They had, of course, played their part by living up to their namesakes by creating merry havoc in town gaining a reputation for themselves as thugs and hooligans but putting that aside, deep within them was the making of good lads.

Gradually Mark explained to them both that they were carrying so much emotional baggage that over time they had become incapable of caring for another's feelings, mainly because they were incapable of caring for themselves. Of course the lads were not receptive to this intensive style of recovery, but somehow they managed to stay on track. Well, that was until they met for one of their last sessions which began as usual by chewing the fat and keeping the conversation nice and shallow. But from nowhere, Mark suggested to them that all of the junk which had gone on in their lives before now was not their fault. Of course they responded like politicians during the late shift with a nonchalant "here! here!" But Mark wasn't interested in pussy footing about and so he continued with the same tact, but this time he moved uncomfortably closer declaring, yet again, that it was not their fault. The atmosphere in the room began to change as the scent of fight or flight danced across the nostrils of anyone who was ready for action. First up, surprisingly, was Darren. A mist of anger had glazed his eyes as he prepared for his usual go-to choice of response, namely his fists. He no longer saw Mark as someone he could trust or respect. No, instead he became the target of his aggression that was about to feel his wrath. But before Darren had the chance to carry out what he thought was his civic duty, Mark was at him first even closer, louder and bolder telling Darren again that none of this was his fault. This outmanoeuvre caught Darren completely off guard and before he knew it, he found himself babbling and crying like a lost child.

The uncomfortable scene unfolding before Frank triggered a flight response and he prepared to exit stage right but again, he too was outmanoeuvred and found his path cut off at the pass by Mark. Frank was met with the same response as Darren, that none of this was his fault. He looked around at his one mate before him, sitting upright on the floor sobbing and then he turned to Mark fully expecting the adrenaline to kick in as he prepared to face his nemesis. Normally the image of that rogue dad from all those years ago would flash through his mind and fuel the rage within- but not this time. No, what played out before him was a scared little boy preparing to run. The memory continued as he relived trying to find his way back home in the dark, which gave him a sense of dread all over again. This time however, his flashback was interrupted by the voice of an annoying little man in a mustard coloured sweatshirt. A colour, by the way that did not suit him as it left him looking washed out. Either way, the voice continued bellowing out that Frank, none of this was your fault and at that moment Frank returned from his flashback and found himself face to face with Mark. He looked at him intently before responding.

"I know it's not Mark. I know it's not."
And then he went over to join his one true friend on the floor and sat with him offering what comfort he could. And that is where Mark left them, both sitting on the floor in a huddle. And as he reached the doorway he turned and gestured a wave.
"See you tomorrow lads" and with that he was gone.

24

2nd Round Qualifying; through by the skin of their teeth

The final whistle blew after six rather long, drawn-out minutes in which Tony, somewhat relieved, later described as more like 6 hours after the near battering into submission by their worthy opponents. Wave after wave of attacks were launched on Clay's rather vulnerable penalty area, as certainly for the last half an hour Handley Park had been penned in and unable to get out of their own half. In fairness, the one nil result in Handley Park's favour did not reflect the sterling efforts made by their opponents, who had outplayed them for best part of the game. If it had not been for one of Clay's special moments, when he launched a pinpoint throw (like the quarterback he once was) some 70 plus yards right onto the diving head of Graham and beyond the keeper, at long last breaking the deadlock, then a replay or possible defeat would have been inevitable.

Later on at a post match briefing, one of the concerns raised was Sam's lack of input and self belief especially in front of goal. You see, right at the beginning of the game, he had squandered at least two or three sitters that should have put the game beyond their opponents but instead it had left the Handley Park players having to dig in and fight hard for the win, leaving them all rather depleted of precious energy. After their briefing, Tony tasked Big Mac and Mark with finding out what on earth was going on with the lad as he seemed pre-occupied, so Mac roped in Clay, to make sure Sam did not feel singled out, and arranged for them all to meet for a bite to eat. Sam, surprisingly, had asked if they wouldn't mind giving Giovannis' a wide berth, using the excuse that he felt a little pasta'd out, so instead they met at a pub on the canal.

To all intents and purposes, Sam seemed fine, engaging in a little banter to fight his manhood corner but once the lads stopped the small talk and started dipping below the surface with a few challenging questions, it became more than apparent that all was not rosy in Sam's garden. After a little more cajoling, Sam finally succumbed and blurted out what was on his mind.

First up was the problems he was experiencing at work. In the last year he had formed a partnership with an old school friend, creating a small firm that specialised in installing approved local authority adaptations in the home that helped those less able and elderly remain, physically, independent for longer. The small firm had been inundated with requests for quotes and subsequent installations, which meant they were now booking up to six months in advance but, for some unknown reason, cash flow was becoming more and more of an issue. This meant purchasing parts to complete work was becoming a problem and for some reason his partner was becoming more and more evasive and a little too vague about what was going in and coming out the business accounts.

Sam just did not get it as figures weren't his strong point but he felt sure there should have been plenty of funds available in the account to cover their overheads, pay their bills and give them both a comfortable standard of living. But instead, Sam was struggling to make ends meet and was becoming more and more reliant on his mum to give him handouts and help keep him financially afloat. He felt embarrassed by it all, after all he was now in his mid twenties and shouldn't have to ask his mum for handouts, especially with all of the hours he was putting in. His partner, on the other hand, seemed far more carefree driving round in a brand new 4x4 pickup, eating out all the time and holidaying like it was going out of fashion. Both Mac and Mark, with slightly raised eyebrows, looked dubiously at each other before responding. But Sam wasn't quite finished with emptying his head of thoughts yet as he had one more problem and for him this was the biggie.

"You see guys, a friend of mine, well, he's kind of sweet on a local girl. In fact, he used to go to school with her back in the day but they have lost contact. Anyway, this friend of mine, he is really keen on her but is slightly worried about her dad."

Again Mac and Mark looked at each other. Clay chipped in.

"Who's the girl?"

But his words fell on deaf ears as Mark launched into the conversation.

"More importantly, who's the mate?"

Sam, slightly flushed, attempted a side step by stating that he was no one they would know as he was an old friend from out of town. Mark jumped in again before the others could.

"So, where do you know him from?"

Again, slightly flustered, Sam attempted to sidestep by saying how they went way back. Finally Mac spoke.

"So, why the issue with the dad?"

Sam swallowed hard before responding "Well, this friend of mine is slightly concerned as the dad is a foreign chap that can be quite fiery at times and maybe a little overprotective."

Mark responded "So what nationality is he?"

Reluctantly Sam responded "Well I'm not sure, but he might be Spanish or maybe Italian!"

Mac, Mark and Clay all looked at each other and started laughing. Sam, trying not to be offended spoke.

"What's so funny? I'm just trying to help a mate out and you lot are laughing at me." Finally Mac spoke "So you're not in love with Giovanni's daughter, Allegra? The same girl you can't stop looking at but are too afraid to speak to and you're worried Giovanni's going to chase you out of town with a blunt instrument."

Sam just looked at them all, initially disgruntled. But soon nodded his head and found himself laughing at himself; partly because he needed to, as he'd been really stressed of late, but also because he knew he was helplessly in love with Allegra; she really was a live wire, and he did not know what to do with himself.

Clay gestured to Sam "So have you spoken with her at all?"

Sam shook his head.

Mark asked "So does she know you even exist?"

Sam responded. "I helped her pick up some broken crockery at the restaurant once and she did say thanks."

There was laughter among the men again before Sam spoke again.

"Maybe I should just forget the whole thing and focus more on work and my football."

Mac was now quick to respond.

"Well, you're right about one thing; you need to get your mind back on your game as you've lost your focus. But let's just take stock for a minute about your work and this business partner of yours as it sounds to me like he is lifting your leg and taking you for a ride."

Sam tried to protest on this one and was about to defend him until he saw the expression on all of the faces of the men he had grown to trust and love over the past year. In an instant he knew they were right and, if truth be told, he'd had an inkling that something was awry but had chosen to ignore it. Maybe it was time to stand tall and challenge his partner about what was really going on with their business. But before he did that, Mark suggested that Sam should meet with a friend of his, who was an accountant. He would be able to help open his eyes a little wider about the state of his business affairs and after that Sam could have his showdown with his soon to be ex-partner, either on his own, or with one or two of the lads to help his partner see the error of his ways.

Big Mac spoke.

"Now we have your soon to-be ex-partner banged to rights, what are we going to do about your love life or lack of?"

Sam winced with embarrassment.

"It's not as simple as that you know? I just get a little tongue-tied when I'm around her, that's all. Back in the day I was always fuelled by booze so engaging with the opposite sex then was no problem. All I had to do was choose a girl that looked as snook-ered as me, so when we attempted to discourse with one another it was easy as neither of us knew what the other was saying."

They all laughed, especially at the thought of Sam under the influence, but it was Clay with his usual heavily accentuated southern twang that spoke.

"Sam if you honestly believe that this is the girl for you, then I would encourage you to pursue her wholeheartedly with every-thing you've got. Spend time with her and get to know her, even if she thinks you're not for her and if at the end of your pursuits she turns you down, then you will be able to accept it purely on the basis that you gave it everything you had."

Nodding approvals from all of the lads left Sam feeling a little better.

"So what's the plan?" asked Mark.

"Well... erm, well, erm, I thought that maybe...." spoke Sam.

"So you have no idea whatsoever?" asked Mark.

"Well, that is a bit harsh as I do have a trick or two up my sleeve" said Sam.

"Like what?" challenged Mark.

Sam started looking at his hands again. "No. I have no idea."

"Well, that's progress. At least you're being honest with yourself. I tell you what. Why don't you leave it with us to arrange an intro and maybe help pave the way with Giovanni? What do you think?" offered Mark.

"Would you mind?" said Sam. "I'd be much obliged to you."

"You leave it to us," said Mac. "Now, let's talk about getting you refocused on your football."

And with that the guys settled in to talk about their next game.

25

A Moral Victory

"How dare he call a man of the cloth 'as shallow as a worm's grave'? I only asked him for some warm-down exercise equipment to help the lads replenish their energy levels." said Mark to Big Mac after his brief meeting with the ever elusive Nigel.

"I think you should count yourself lucky that you even achieved an audience with him considering his hectic schedule of busy doing nothing 24 hours a day!" pronounced Mac.

The men's clenched knuckles nonchalantly met in the air, in response to their good comebacks regarding Nigel's lack of concern for the welfare of the players of Handley Park Rangers. It just seemed like every time you asked for something that involved a little time or effort or a slight investment, then he was on his toes and gone; like a rat up a drainpipe. Although morale was at an all time high since the introduction of the new management team, you could tell that tempers were starting to fray. Salaries were not being met at all, let alone on time, and from the whispers in the corridors amongst the skeleton office staff, it would appear that overdue bills were starting to stack up along with the list of demands for payments on account. Mark had chosen to tackle Nigel regarding some new equipment, fully aware that Nigel would palm him off with some lame excuse about club priorities and looking at the bigger picture, but for Mark the anticipated response did not matter. You see, he had his own agenda as the request for equipment was no more than a smoke screen. What he wanted was access to an old dilapidated portacabin that used to house the match officials on match day but had not been used for many years.To all intents and purposes it was uninhabitable, which was the sole reason why Nigel agreed for it to be used in the hope of side stepping the annoying chaplain. But what Nigel thought was a good wild goose chase to occupy Mr. Goody Two Shoes, was in fact the exact opportunity Mark was looking for- to help alleviate the atmosphere created by the wake of broken promises created by the aforementioned Nigel Hawkson.

 Mark had a network of contacts and friends, along with acquaintances across the town and much further afield, that he had established over the many years of pastoring the local community. In fact, Mark had friends in very high places and was fully aware of the goings-on concerning Nigel's business affairs, or lack of. He was also aware of Nigel's secret shady deal to offload the club to an offshore property developer in the hope of bringing down the curtain on Handley Park Rangers once and for all. Unbeknown to Nigel, Mark, through some of his business contacts, had arranged for the deal to be buried within the appropriations team of the local town council's building regulations department, with the express aim of scuppering the deal. He believed it was not good for business right now, especially as things were on the up!

Nigel, not requiring any excuses to vacate the building, left pretty sharpish. He felt satisfied that he had laid down the law with Mark regarding unnecessary equipment, whilst at the same time relenting quite happily to the use of the old prefab building as it represented no value to him at all. So with Nigel's blessing, Mark took to task the old building with the express aim of scoring a rather large motivational goal to all concerned at the club. With the slightly rusty and twisted key now in his possession, Mark began to hatch his plan of remodelling the old prefab unit and creating a makeshift oasis of tranquillity and calm, which was something they could all do with right now. Both Tony and Big Mac had been kept out of the picture, being told by Mark that he intended to use the space for a little storage. The only assistance Mark had called upon was Sam, due to his expertise with plumbing and building work. You see, after a recent heart-to-heart with Sam, Mark had let slip about his idea of adding a warm down zone at the club to help the players recover their strength and agility with a little more zeal. The piece de resistance fell into place when Sam mentioned that he had access to an old hot tub that was no longer required by one of his clients and just needed disposing of.

The tub, although tired from years of use, was in pretty good condition and surprisingly deep for its size. Sam seemed to believe that he could easily revive it with an overhaul and a little TLC and if Mark wanted use of it then he would have it up and running in no time at all, ready for action. Mark did not need asking twice and soon set Sam to work installing the hot tub and even had him sinking the tub within the sub-floor just to add a little touch of class to its new home. Next on the agenda were the ice baths. Well, they weren't actually ice baths; more commercial chest deep freezers from a local grocery store that was in the middle of a refit. Mark had managed to appropriate them at no cost, along with a lifetime supply of ice to help keep the players muscles in check. Again, with the help of Sam they had managed to sink and convert them within the subfloor to create 3 ice baths that now only required their victim's presence to complete the look. Between them they even managed to hot seam weld an Aquarius non-slip vinyl throughout even into 6 new shower areas complete with clean, hot running water. Sam had noted that all they were missing was a sauna or spa area to complete the look but found himself corrected when Mark mentioned that an old friend of his wanted to dispose of an old Finnish sauna that hadn't been used for many years and was in need of repair. The old care home, where the sauna lived, had closed its doors some two years back. Mark had spent many a night there listening to stories of old with some of its occupants, including one of Brian Hawkson's old buddies from the war. After a brief chat on the phone, Mark had been granted access to the sauna on the proviso that it was carefully removed without causing any internal damage to the property. Again with Sam's help, the old Finnish sauna was dismantled and re-assembled in its new lavish home at Handley Park Rangers. In less than a month, the work was complete, which came as a relief to Sam as he was keen to start earning a wage again. The two men surveyed the room and were both impressed with its interior, complete with several planters throughout the place. They had purposely left the exterior in its original state so as not to create any interest from prying eyes, but the inside? Wow! It was truly amazing and when both Tony and Mac, along with the rest of the squad, were invited to view they could not believe the transformation.

"Where on earth did all of this equipment come from?" asked Tony. "No, don't tell me; one of Mark's acquaintances?" but no response was forth coming from either Mark or Sam.

Tony continued "I don't know how you have done this but, wow, it is amazing! I'm guessing Nigel did not sanction this or is even aware of what you have done?"

Both men just smirked and shrugged their shoulders.

"Ok, well let's just keep it that way and make sure the squad makes the most of those ice baths, especially after one of your epic challenging runs," he suggested. "Oh, and thanks boys, that's a real boost for us right now. I really appreciate it. Now who can we entice to try out the new ice baths?"

And with that everyone turned round looking towards Big Mac.

"Oh no don't look at me!" commanded Mac "You should never look like that at a bloke who's been trained in the use of weaponry!" With that, he was on his toes heading out of the room and across the floodlit pitch closely followed by the entire squad. Tony turned to Mark suggesting that "I don't much fancy his chances tonight."

"Oh, I wouldn't worry about him too much. He can be pretty ruthless when necessary, especially at the thought of an ice bath waiting for him" replied Mark and with that the two men strolled out into the cool night air to watch the commotion unfold.

26

You're live on air with HP radio again. Radio interview with Nigel Hawkson and Charles Hayworth.

Charles show host: "And now let's give a big hand for the owner of the team of the moment. Our very own Handley Park Rangers. Welcome once again Nigel Hawkson."

Nigel: "Always a pleasure Charles. You know that!"

Charles: "Thanks Nigel, I guess it is", expressed rather dubiously.

Nigel: "I've always been an advocate for supporting local business; you know be vocal, buy local and all that sort of thing, what! Especially our local radio show, HP on air!"

Charles: "You must be so proud of the team right now, sitting top 5 in the league and almost through the qualifying rounds for the first time in club history I do believe".

Nigel: "Yes our boys are doing well, I am pleased".

Charles: "Your late father, Brian, must be looking down on you all right now, a very proud man."

Nigel: slight cough of irritation. "I don't know about all that

Charles but I am satisfied with the progress my team is making".

Charles: "You must be thrilled with Tony Jeff's surprising success, especially with no former track record. His leadership and management style are receiving much attention and praise. He really is the man of the moment"

Nigel: slightly clipped. "Tony is progressing exactly how I wanted him to when I first took a chance on him".

Charles: "But surely Nigel you must be thrilled with the way he has guided the team not only out of the relegation zone but now as possible title contenders!"

Nigel: "Let's not get too carried away, hey. It is just a case of right time, right place. You know that Charles and don't forget Mike Phillips and the legacy he has left behind."

Charles: "Surely you're not crediting Mike Phillips for the success of the team right now. From what I hear Mike had very little input even when he was at the helm. "

A rather disgruntled **Nigel**: "Now you're crossing the line Charles. I'm neither crediting nor discrediting the works of our previous manager. I'm just pointing out a fact."

Charles: Now trying a different tact! "How about financial commitment and rewards Nigel? Surely you must be enjoying the fruits of a the next round especially with a tie at home?"

Nigel starting to get a little out of his pram: "I'm not here Charles to discuss the finances of my football club! You of all people should know that!"

Charles: "Oh sorry Nigel I didn't mean to pry about the club finances but surely you must now be able to consider some much needed home ground improvements given the sorry state of your late father's precious Hawker Tempest stand".

Nigel with toys now being thrown from his pram: "Again I say to you I am not here to discuss the club finances."

Charles: (Getting into the swing of things now) "Sorry to hear you say that Nigel as I'm led to believe there are still first team players who have not received an income for months. Can you confirm or deny that?"

Nigel, now standing with arms gesticulating all over the shop: "I don't need to inform you Charles that this interview is now over!"

Charles: "Oh come on Nigel don't be such a spoil sport. I'm sorry to hear you say that as our listeners were lining up some very interesting questions to ask you"

Infuriated Nigel storms out of the studio and slams the door as he exits.

Charles: "Well there you have it folks. Handley Park Rangers, a club potentially going places with an owner not prepared to show off his team or disclose the future plans or vision of our local club. What a shame; either way let's make a big effort for the up and coming game by supporting our boys."Come on you Home Guard!"

27

Nigel starting to lose control of Handley Park Rangers (at long last)

"I think we have to assume that there is some truth in what our man tells us and that Nigel has scarpered, probably to sunnier climates taking with him the clubs winnings to date" advised Big Mac.

"Which leaves us flat broke and up a rather long creek without a paddle" added Mark for poetic licence. The room fell silence for a time before Tony asked

"Who else knows about this?"

"I think it's fair to say that the players are pretty much up to speed given the fact that they have not received a salary for the best part of 6 months, coupled with the fact that anything with any value has been lifted by our local friendly bailiffs just for good measure" chipped in Mac.

"The local radio are all over it; enjoying the rumours and doing their utmost to add a little petrol to the fire," commented Mark.

"Yeah I thought that was the case," confirmed Tony.

"So what's the plan?" asked Mac looking to Tony.

"To tell you the truth guys, just between us, I have no idea but one thing is for sure. There's no way I'm letting that douche off the hook with this and I refuse to let this club go under for his selfish endeavour. Not on my watch!" warned Tony as he banged his fist on the desk.

"Listen guys," began Mark. "You might not like what I'm about to tell you but just bear with me for a minute".

Both Tony and Big Mac looked at each other quizzically.

"I was pretty sure Nigel was up to no good and I'd heard through the grapevine that he was scheming to offload the club to the highest bidder. He was also looking to ensure the club could not sustain its losses, hoping that it would close its doors for the last time," continued Mark. "In fact he'd received a substantial offer in principle from some shady property developers for a handsome profit but I asked a friend of mine in the local council to bury the change of use applications within the planning department which soon put paid to that. But what I did not realise was that Nigel had squandered the initial sweetener or small coffee as they like to call it, imparted to him in a rather large brown envelope," cautioned Mark. "Now, that was a game changer as it seemed to push him further out on a ledge. He no longer seemed interested in covering his tracks and from that moment on his actions were pretty much blatant. Don't you remember the last time he was challenged by accounts about when cheques would be released for payment to both creditors and staff and he just told her to keep her nose out of his affairs?" noted Mark.

"Well I just thought he was his usual stressed out self!" goaded Mac.

"Go figure," pronounced Tony.

"Well, I can only apologise for not sharing this information with you sooner as I thought it best at the time to have you guys focus solely on your football. I guess I was hoping to out manoeuvre

Nigel further down the line before things got too out of hand," proclaimed Mark. "Do you know he owes money just about everywhere? The local casino, the bookies – all three of them - a rather large slate at a wine bar in town. Even his car was on tick and the finance house are already in the process of repossessing within the next month," warned Mark.

"Wow! There is no way that I could lead my life like that and sleep at night!" retorted Mac.

"Me neither," agreed Tony.

"So what now?" asked Mac.

Glazed looks with puffed out cheeks appeared as the men fell silent.

"Well, I do have one final trick up my sleeve, which you may or may not want to hear" cautioned Mark.

"Well, let's have it!" chimed in Tony.

"Have either of you heard of a man called Mr. K Samson, a successful local businessman with a rather impressive rags to riches story?" asked Mark.

Both men showed no recognition of the story.

"Well, I happen to know Mr. Samson rather well as I have been involved in his path to recovery over the last few years. In fact, I introduced him to an investor friend of mine to help him get his business venture off the ground. Anyway long story short, his dot com business exploded and Mr. Samson never looked back," confirmed Mark.

"And you are telling us this because?" enquired Tony.

"Oh sorry," conceded Mark. "You see he is keen to give back and invest within the local community and I may well have mentioned the possibility of an investment opportunity at Handley Park Rangers."

"You know, for a man of the cloth you really know how to duck and dive!" snickered Mac.

"Now you are starting to hurt my feelings!" retorted Mark.

Tony glared at Mac. "Carry on Mark," he motioned.

"He genuinely wants to help and is waiting for the opportunity," advised Mark.

"Why the sudden interest in Handley Park Rangers and why do I get the feeling you are not telling us everything?" chirped in Mac.

"Well I may have inadvertently forgotten to mention one point, but I will come to that. Don't forget though, that part of the reason for the interest in us is obvious as we are the star attraction in the town right now," Mark said.

"Yeah, but there's still a "but" in there somewhere, I can feel it in my waters!" urged Tony.

Mark coughed nervously. "Well, he does happen to have a bit of history with one of our players," coughed Mark.

"Go on," added Mac.

"Who's the player?" asked Tony.

"Graham," confirmed Mark.

"And where does he know him from?" asked Mac.

"The City shopping mall from back in the day when he was homeless," advised Mark.

"And the first name?" demanded Mac.

"Mr. Kieran Samson; managing director of Dronenet," commented Mark.

"Not the Kieran that helped end a rather special career and leave a man's life in tatters?" challenged Tony.

"Guilty as charged," blurted Mark.

All three men looked intently at each other and said nothing for a while. Big Mac rubbed the stubble across his chin back and forth under his jaw line before circling the back of his fingers in an anti-clockwise motion around his mouth.

Mac spoke first "What do you think Tony?"

"Now that's a tough one Mac," replied Tony "but in fairness to you Mark, I think you've done a sterling job in the background, if not a little unorthodox at times, but you've had our back and for that I'm truly grateful. In a month of Sundays I would never have guessed what Nigel was up to. Oh, don't get me wrong I knew he was as shallow as a worm's grave and that his life solely evolved around him, but to clear the business accounts of all of the hard earned cash that these guys have accumulated? And for what? No wonder he'd recently taken an interest in trying to coax Sam and Graham to consider career moves to more highly ranked clubs, he was just trying to feather his own nest. All to line his own pockets and there was me thinking that maybe he had turned over a new leaf," uttered Tony.

"So where do we go from here Tony?" exclaimed Mac.

Tony squeezed the arms of his chair, stood and grabbed a stale coffee from the pot. "Listen up guys. This is how I see us moving forward!" declared Tony. "Mac, I want you to go see Graham and explain all that is going on. I need you to spin one of your special- forces stories and make it fit, concerning how Graham will move forward from this moment on and remember to let him know that he is not alone in this," added Tony. "Mark, I need you to arrange for Kieran to come in and meet with me, initially, followed by a meeting with the three of us," he continued. "We need to gauge that this guy is for real, as we have no room for error here. And Mark, I need you to try and find out where the scarlet pimpernel is so we can contact him. If he realises that we can find him, then it might just unnerve him enough to realise that others can too and that may just be the bargaining tool we need to get the right result."

"And what result might that be?" asked Mac.

"To get our club back guys. Don't you see it? It's our club; the towns' and the people of this town and it's about time Mr. Hawkson knew that!" roared Tony. "You guys up for it?"

In unison both men replied "Definitely!"

"Good," confirmed Tony. "Now one last thing. Let's use this whole debacle to our advantage."

"But how?" inquired Mac.

"Them and us!" hinted Tony. "Works every time. People keep taking from us. Life tries to keep sticking it to us. Between us, we don't have two ha'pennies to rub together and to the rest of the footballing- world we must look like a laughing stock and that, gentlemen, is exactly where I want to be right now."

"Care to elaborate a little on that?" requested Mark.

"All in good time guys but remember this for now; we are playing from a position of strength, not weakness, and that this situation is the exact catalyst we need right now that will push us to the next level," challenged Tony.

"I'd better go see Graham then," stated Mac.

"Once you've done that Mac, let's arrange to meet with all of the players and staff and have it out with them; warts and all," suggested Tony.

"And I'll go get Kieran and then see if I can't give that scarlet pimpernel a few sleepless nights," put in Mark.

"That's the ticket," encouraged Tony. "See you guys later. I'm off on a date night! Fish and chips for one with a full fat coke if I'm lucky at this rate."

"Sounds a gourmet delight," laughed Mark. "Enjoy".

"Thanks guys I'll see you tomorrow," and with that he was gone.

"What do you reckon to that?" Mark said to Mac.

"It's crazy of course but I think he's right and if anyone can pull this off it's us right now," replied Mac.

"Me too," offered Mark. "Now, what special- forces story are we going to talk about?" .

But all he received as a response from Mac was a slight tap to the side of his nose and with that both men left for the night.

28

Half time team talk – Time to gatecrash the party!

Nobody needed reminding just how important today's game was, especially as they were one match away from the 1st round proper. Most tier 8 non-league clubs would have given their left arm for an opportunity like this. The team were competing in the largest stadium and in front of the most hostile crowd to date. They knew the game plan inside and out as Big Mac had drummed it into them week in week out; keep it simple and let the ball do the work. Keep the ball on the ground and play to feet. Sit back, absorb the pressure and expect the opposition to maintain their usual high percentage of ball possession but look for any given opportunity to take them on the counter especially if the big man in the sticks sees a gap opening up.

They expected a large crowd, but were a little surprised at their hostility, naively assuming that as an underdog, their presence would be overlooked but not this crowd -   they were in fine fettle! As Handley Park were from football's lower reaches, they were also aware that the team they were facing were 4 divisions higher, therefore probably fitter, more tactically minded and more skilful with the ball. But as Big Mac put it, "Chances are they'll be missing one vital ingredient lads; the professional's code of honour – they just don't want it enough!"

The half time whistle had just blown, so the lads made their way through the tunnel and into the visitor's dressing room where they slumped down onto the teak bench seats below their soft-close lockers. The floor, heated from below, was solid and professionally tiled using a warm Mexican terracotta mosaic rather than the hollow, slightly bowed floor the team were used to, that flexed beneath your feet every time you moved around the Pacemaker portakabin. The lads were frustrated and were starting to waiver in the belief that they should stick to their game plan. One of them even kicked his bottle of energy drink across the floor to the showers in frustration.

Although they weren't losing, truth be told they certainly weren't winning. They just could not seem to get out of their half and were yet to achieve a shot at their opponent's goal. To them right now it just wasn't working and their flow of play was being stifled and snuffed out every time they tried to build any form of momentum.

Tony instinctively knew he had a job to do. His team were on edge and the tell-tale signs of bickering were starting to creep in. Big Mac had also picked up on the tension but knew full well that the strength of character and leadership required right now had to come from the man standing before them all. Tony took a deep breath and raised both his arms vertically and stretched out his palms at the same time raising his shoulders and tilting his head to one side and then the other. He looked as if he was preparing for some sort of Olympic WR attempt but instead he had other plans on his mind. Mark looked up intrigued wondering what was about to happen.

"You know guys," claimed Tony "over the years many inspiring leaders have challenged, cajoled and motivated their men and women with anecdotes and words of wisdom in the hope of changing mindsets and, of course, the historic outcome of their given sport or subject matter. I believe, of course, that now is the time for us as men to step up to the plate and deliver if we are going to live up to our destiny. But essentially, and more importantly right now, we need to remedy our lack of belief because I feel this team has lost something today".

He looked across to Big Mac and Mark whilst giving a knowing wink before moving his gaze towards the rest of the team. Looking them squarely in the eyes he continued

"I believe that we as a team have lost that running feeling."

Big Mac looked at Mark and then closed his eyes and shook his head. He covered his mouth with his hand as Tony continued. Each player looked round at each other starring slightly aghast as Tony, wholeheartedly took centre stage of the dressing room and much louder this time declared that the chaps had lost that running feeling. Knowing full well what was coming Big Mac sighed, put both hands on his knees and looked at Tony totally bemused. Tony looked right back at Mac and then Mark challenging them this time and announced

"Yes they have, Big Mac!"

Big Mac looked down at the floor whilst the team looked on in utter bewilderment. Finally, there came a response from Big Mac as he reluctantly nodded in agreement with Tony before standing to his feet and turning to join his friend and colleague. Side by side, they took a deep intake of breath before making a short "ahem" grunting sound as first Tony burst into song with

"You never close your mouth anymore when I miss free kicks."

Shortly followed by Big Mac with

"And there's no tendinitis like before in your knees or hips."

Then together in unison with football boots as makeshift microphones,

"You're trying hard not to show boat, baby. But maybe, maybe you'll go for it."

At that moment Mark felt a nudge on his shoulder and was quickly asked by Sam; "I'm not so sure about those lyr...." but before he had a chance to finish his sentence Mark cut him short by suggesting that it was probably best that he did not go there.

To be brutally honest, the sound wasn't particularly good and the likes of Ed Sheeran or James May should have no fear for their future careers but, in the main, it had the desired effect as virtually all of the players were on their feet joining their coaches and as one voice they continued.

"You've lost that running' feelin' Whoa, that running' feelin', you've lost that running' feelin'. Now it's gone....gone....gone.... woah."

By the time they reached the second verse, Mark had everyone joining in including the stragglers and their raised voices could now be heard echoing through the corridors, offices and changing areas. In fact, the coach of the opposing team was midway through his half time team talk, letting his players know just how pathetic their efforts had been thus far, when he stopped in his tracks and straightened his back to listen to what was going on.

When their song finally petered out the final woah, woah, woah and the boom, boom, boom, boom, boom, boom, boom, boom hummed away into the distance, the guys just looked at each other laughing and high fiving and hugging. Tony now looked at his squad and declared

"Our work here is done!"

Not only were the players now unified but also ignited with a burning fire to get the job done. As the guys stood and mentally prepared for the 2nd half of their cup tie, there was no more fear or doubt or unbelief or failure. These men of simple means were on a mission and they intended to keep that burning desire of belief alive.

Big Mac now took his place before the team and declared "You know the game plan, you've held this team off for best part of an hour. Now it's your turn to turn the tables on them. Let's switch places and take the game to them. They've had their chance, now you do it, let's finish the job!"

The team roared their approval and were soon led out for the 2nd half. As the team exited, Big Mac turned to Tony and insisted "I do hate it when you do that!"

"Do what?" echoed Tony grinning.

"You know exactly what!" grimaced Mac and continued "Do you know, if you had asked me six months ago, 'could this team make it through the 1st round qualifying?' I would have told you no, no way! But if you were to ask me now could we make it to the 1st round proper then I would say' definitely maybe'."

Tony just looked at Big Mac and responded by saying "You can forget the 1st round proper."

Mac replied "What? Don't you believe the lads can achieve this Tony?"

"No I don't" retorted Tony. "I believe they can go all the way!"

"What! You're not serious?" challenged Mac.

"No," replied Tony. "I'm deadly serious."

The men, now joined by Mark, turned and followed their players out onto the pitch. "You know Tony," insisted Mac "you are a very dangerous man at times. In fact you're plain crazy off the charts!"

"I know Mac." chuckled Tony as he reached over and extended

an arm across Mac's shoulders. "That's why I need a navigator like you, along with Mark to keep me on track and in check."

"You certainly do," chipped in Mark entering the dugout.

"What's that?" asked one of the players.

"Oh, I was just telling Tony what a lunatic he is" confided Mac.

"I could have told you that" boomed the player. "Anyone of us could have told you that!" and with that the player continued his conversation with his teammate on the bench.

29

It's time to shoot that big elephant in the room

"So I'm not in trouble Big Mac?" asked Graham as they sat at a corner table in a local coffee house.

"No, of course not son! Why would you think that?" affirmed Mac.

"I don't know, I guess you just make me nervous, especially when we go for a quick chat that's all," replied Graham apprehensively. "You're not trying to move me on though are you as Nigel did mention there could be some possibilities for me to explore?"

"Look, you're not in trouble and no one is out to sell you, well not anymore" declared Big Mac, adding the last bit under his breath, as he cupped his flat white, decaf with soya whilst at the same time, trying not to disturb the pattern of his favourite barista florette. He soon turned his attention to his rather large chocolate teacake before continuing

"Look son," Mac paused for a minute before finally launching straight in with it. "There is no easy way to say this so I'm just going to say it anyway. Remember some time ago, the homeless man you stopped to help and in doing so things kind of got a little out of hand and, well you know the rest," commented Mac. "Well, he's come out of the woodwork recently and has been in touch with the club." Graham stood up nervously. His face shone like a rabbit in the headlight beam of a moving car.

"Well, say something!" challenged Mac.

"You don't mean Kieran do you?" stammered a rather nervous Graham.

Big Mac nodded.

"He can't have as I'm still not even sure that he exists, you see, it's as if that part of my life never happened," implored Graham. "One minute he was there and then he just disappeared into thin air. The whole thing just didn't seem real." He sat down again fumbling with the buttons on his jacket.

"This lad is really carrying some stuff," thought Mac to himself." It is as if he is scared of his own shadow."

Mac continued to listen to Graham as he retold the tale that seemed to be stranded in his mind and what made it worse, he kept referring to it as the worst experience anyone could ever have imagined. Mac knew that Mark had spent a lot of time helping Graham rebuild not just his health, but his life as well, but he had no idea how stuck this young man was with this past experience. Yes, of course it was a life changing moment and at such a young age, but there comes a time in a young man's life when he needs to break the chains of doubt and fear and move on with his journey, even if it is only an inch at a time. But to Mac, the impression he had of Graham right now was that the lad was quite happy staying put where he was.

Mac had heard just about enough moaning and groaning for one day! Coupled with the fact that his flat white had gone cold, he'd had to share some of his teacake with a boisterous toddler running up and down the line of comfy seats that stretched the full length of the cafe, and for Mac, that just wasn't cricket! Finally Graham finished his story of woe and to be truthful it was pretty traumatic.

Mac leaned in to Graham "Well done for sharing lad. It couldn't have been easy going back there but you did." He took an intake of breath and again leaned in as he wanted the lad's full attention. "Listen, I want to share a story which I think may help you. You up for it?" He asked earnestly. Graham looked Mac in the eyes and nodded. "I agree life isn't always pink and fluffy. It can be tough sometimes and we can end up taking different paths, paths we never anticipated but that's just the way it is," continued Mac. "As you probably know, I was in the armed forces for best part of 20 years; man and boy you could say. It brought the best out in me and, at times, the worst for that matter but one experience I'm about to share was one of those defining moments that can change the course of your life. Of the 20 years as a soldier I spent just over 12 of them in Special Forces. For many of the men it became their identity as they considered themselves the elite, the pick of the crop, the crème de la crème of the covert ops world, but not me. You see for me, it was all about the challenge; strategizing situations down to the Nth degree and overcoming all the obstacles that were thrown at us," advised Mac. "It was never on a whim, no, it was calculated and controlled; that was the discipline. Anyway, one particular mission I was behind enemy lines in civvies and tasked with disrupting communications for a local faction that were creating a right merry havoc in what was fast becoming one of the most dangerous cities in the world," Mac continued. "Three days into the mission, I was travelling with two men in a clapped out vehicle that broke down right in the middle of a busy highway. There was no way of repairing the vehicle as it was on its last legs but we had to move quickly as we would soon draw attention to ourselves and my fake tan probably wouldn't have stood up to too much scrutiny," Mac said laughing to himself. "So we ever so politely asked a cabbie if we could borrow his vehicle for a time." Graham looked at Mac quizzically. "I can be quite persuasive especially when pointing a weapon up someone's left nostril," he laughed again. Graham shifted in his seat at the thought of Mac with a gun. "Anyway, we managed to get mobile and were soon on our way knowing that within the hour we would be at our first rendezvous," he continued. "Turns out our friendly cabbie must have taken umbrage to us borrowing his cab and had somehow managed to communicate a message ahead, as, before we knew it, we were soon surrounded by some rather zealous looking soldiers and consequently we were taken. No one had any idea where we were and we had no way of making contact with anyone. We were stripped bare of possessions, including our clothes, and then followed the process of them obtaining information whilst doing their utmost to break our hearts and minds," claimed Mac rather coldly. "Anyway, no amount of training can prepare you for that; it's just you and your tormentors and, to be honest, they weren't giving up any time soon," he continued. "Days became weeks and weeks soon became months and before I knew it, the year was gone. By then I was holding on to life by a shoestring, it was a really ugly moment for me." There was a pause in the conversation as Mac seemed to disappear with his thoughts to some distant past. At one point Graham considered nudging Mac to try and bring him back but soon thought better of it. Instead he sat and waited patiently for Mac to return which inevitably he did. Mac, now back in the room looked down at his hands that were shaking uncontrollably and quickly attempted to disguise the fact by shaking himself in his seat a little and stretching before taking a gulp of his drink. "Anyway," he continued. "Where was I?" "Ah, yes! Miraculously, by some form of divine intervention my location became of interest to my unit and before long, demands were made for my return and after some careful negotiations I was repatriated with my team," Mac paused to see Graham looking totally shocked.

Graham stuttered a little before eventually stringing a sentence together; "How did you cope afterwards?"

"I didn't," divulged Mac. "I lasted no more than another 8 months on active duty before overstepping the mark whilst on tour somewhere in Egypt and before I knew it I was politely asked to consider a career change. That's when my whole world came crashing down around me. Civvy street beckoned and the only support I was offered back then was a 5 minute "how are you doing?" chat which finished with me being given some vitamins to help me through." Mac shook his head whilst laughing to himself again. "Listen son, it took me a long time to deal with the civil war that was raging within me but the question has to be the same for you as it was for me back then. 'Do you get better or bitter trying again?' What's it to be" asked Mac looking seriously now at Graham. "For a long time I questioned what was real or fiction during my whole ordeal. I questioned the injustice of a human being treating another in such a manner and I have to say I questioned, on many occasion, my own sanity," admitted Mac keen to strike a chord within Graham's own thought process.

The two men sat in silence for awhile, Mac knowing for sure that now was the time for him to remain silent and allow Graham some time to think before responding.

"Mac, I had no idea about this and I can't begin to fathom what you went through and how on earth you managed to come out the other side," stated Graham.

"Oh that's easy," affirmed Mac. "You breathe in and out every day and keep wading through the bad days until eventually you start enjoying the odd day. Then finally life becomes more colourful again... plus you rely on crazy characters like Mark and Tony to help get you through," laughed Mac.

"Now that I can relate to," chuckled Graham and both men laughed at the thought of their familiar "Running man" doing what he does best when it comes to men dealing with emotional turmoil.

"Where did you meet Mark?" asked Graham.

Mac's face attempted to disguise a grimace before he spoke "Oh, that's a story for another time." Moving on quickly he continued "So Graham, where do we go from here? Is it the wide path of mediocrity with you continuing to hide yourself away at the slightest sound of trouble, or shall we take the narrow path of strength and bust out of here?"

"Will you help me Mac?" asked Graham earnestly, as he contemplated his options.

"No," affirmed Mac, "we all will. Now I believe it is time you were properly introduced to the man who allegedly ruined your life because from where I'm sitting, I see a young man with a bright future ahead of him and just maybe in the months ahead, given time, you might just see the same as me," boasted Mac.

"Thanks Mac for this," offered Graham.

"No, thank you son! This time for me; with you and the rest of our motley crew, along with those two crazy men at the helm, this is fast becoming one heck of a ride for me and for that I'm truly grateful," replied Mac. And with that, the two men stood and without giving it a second thought, they embraced as two men who had stared life in the face and come out the other side fighting.

30

Kieran Samson

"Welcome to Handley Park Rangers Mr. Samson," advised Tony as they shook hands warmly and took a brief moment to weigh each other up.

"It's a pleasure to be here, do call me Kieran."

"Thanks and likewise I'm Tony, please take a seat," and both men grabbed a seat on an old fashioned worn out leather sofa that had seen better days. Tony kick started the conversation "I have to say Kieran, your interest in Handley Park Rangers does come as a complete shock not only to me but, of course will be to Graham as well."

"I know," commented Kieran. "I can't begin to understand how Graham will feel when he hears about me, but I must let you understand that my intentions are honourable. I just want to help put things right."

"And if you can't?" asked Tony. "I have one of the coaches spending time with him at the moment, breaking the news gently ,I hope, and trying to help him process things." .

"It's a chance I'm willing to take, as his actions back then not only saved my life but they inspired me back from the brink. I owe him so much and my understanding from Mark is Graham has the opportunity to reach his true potential under your guidance," continued Kieran.

"It's not my guidance Kieran, as the way I see it is we are a unit of men on a mission," stated Tony.

"So I hear and I would like to help you with that," offered Kieran.

"Good, so how would you like to get involved?" asked Tony.

"Well, firstly by looking at where I can financially help to keep the club afloat. But in the long term, I have some ideas concerning how the club can move forward as a community benefit society" suggested Kieran.

"A community what?" asked Tony.

"Ah a friend of mine has recently been involved in the regeneration of a club whereby they initiated a community benefit society. This involved raising funds by shared ownership to the amount acceptable to the club creditors and in return, the community received the majority shareholding along with the benefit of a democratic decision making process" advised Kieran.

"Now that sounds really interesting as we have a number of issues to contend with here. At present, for example, the players have not been paid in well over 6 months, suppliers no longer supply and maintenance of the club is just about non-existent," confided Tony.

"Well, if you would allow me I would love to help" noted Kieran with real intensity.

Tony thought for a while before responding "Can you leave it with me Kieran? I would like to discuss with my management team, plus I need to take into account how Graham is with all of this and, of course, I need to work out what can be done about the present owner of the club."

"That is absolutely fine with me" added Kieran "and I fully understand if you decide to not take me up on my offer but do allow me to reiterate one last time the sincerity of its intent," and with that the two men again shook hands before parting.

Tony always relied on the intuitive instinct that had served him well many times over the years and right now, his instinct was telling him to grab that hand of help with all of his might. But he also knew that he must discuss this with his team and more importantly, be satisfied that Graham was able to cope with the demons from his past. Only time could tell how that story was going to unravel.

31

Mind games

Tony, Big Mac and Mark sat at their familiar table in their local Italian cafe waiting for Tony's usual turkey Milanese, served up on a bed of prosciutto and fontina, topped off with a fried egg. Off course Mac & Mark couldn't see the appeal as they would have much preferred a good old fashioned fry-up. But Tony, being Tony, was not one to accept defeat when trying to improve the palate of his two brothers-in-arms, although sometimes you are best off not trying in the first place even if your favourite Italian family from Minori just off the Amalfi coast are cooking for you.

Giovanni, the cafe owner and avid Handley Park Rangers stalwart supporter, had followed the fortunes of the club for as long as he could remember. He briefly joined them for coffee and with a heavy accentuated tone he said "You know I thought that a things could a not get any worse in our beautiful game after the longa drawn out debacle with football's governing body concerning all the bribes, the corruption and the lies. But then, a blow me down, I come across this story about a head coach," Giovanni continued whilst shaking his head. "You know, I really thought that things were about to change for the better when I saw the genuine passion and excitement expressed in his voice about obtaining his dream job, and then this happens".

"You know what I think?" Mac cut in.

"That it's a greed that is the fuel in the fire that is a killing the game?" Giovanni replied.

"No, well yes in a way, but in the main its people selling themselves short of their integrity and for what? A few extra quid in their pocket?" he suggested whilst gesticulating with his arms in the air. "When is enough, enough?"

Tony jumped in "You know, my old dad always used to say that it is not that money is the route of all evil, but that it is the love of money that is the route of all evil, and that certainly seems to ring as true today as it did back then."

The men nodded in agreement. Giovanni laughed to himself and continued "You know people should treat a money like it is the horse manure. It is of no value if you pile it up high, but if we were to only spread it around a little well then maybe that is when a the miracle a begins and we see the things starting to grow," and this time all of the men began to laugh.

Giovanni stood up slowly and gradually straightened his back. He was an old man now but still possessed a spring in his step and a twinkle in his eye. "How are the boys a doing?" he asked. "How are they feeling about Nigel's disappearance?"

"Well, in the main it makes no difference as he was never there in the first place and if he was, he was nothing but a pain in the backside," mocked Mac.

"Our only concern is keeping everything afloat and everyone together as no one has been paid for such a long time," added Mark.

"It is a miracle that everyone has stayed together for so long," confided Mac.

Giovanni shook his head "No, everyone a stays put because of you men. They play a because of you and they play a so well because of you," he stated with such emotion.

"You looking for some sort of a tip?" contributed Mac.

"Fat a chance of that if you are paying the bill!" Giovanni challenged in response.

The men laughed again and Giovanni discreetly left them as he could tell they had plenty on their mind and needed to talk.

Mark spoke first looking to Tony "So, what did you think of Kieran?"

Tony dabbed his mouth with a serviette and drank some coffee. "Well, you're right Mark, I like him and think he is sincere in his desire to do all he can to assist the club." Mac cut in "We don't need another member of our management team, we just need a little help to steer us through our financial dilemma."

Mark responded "We shouldn't even be sitting here talking about financial frailty not with all of the money this team has earned so far this year."

"I know," commented Mark "and yet here we are!"

The men all looked at each other as they could all sense an air of frustration.

"But we have a life line do we not?" confirmed Mark.

"Yes we do" added Tony "and I believe he will be the man that can salvage this place." "With no strings attached?" tested Mac.

"Yeah and with no strings attached" confided Tony. "By the way! Have any of you ever heard of a community benefit society?" he asked. But before anyone could respond he added "Scratch that. I'm jumping ahead of myself. It's just that someone mentioned a possible way of taking control of the club and giving it back to the people. It's something we can look into another time." Realising that he'd been in deep conversation with himself he looked at the blank faces in front of him and quickly steered the men's focus towards Graham and whether he would be able to cope with the re-emergence of Kieran.

There were interesting times ahead for the club. With so many balls in the air, it was difficult for the three of them to keep their focus on the football, especially with a difficult game ahead with their neighbouring footballing giants across the county in their state of the art, 30 000- seater stadium.

"Has their coach commenced the usual mind games yet?" Mac asked Tony

"Oh, he started with the wind ups as soon as our name was pulled out of the velvet bag," observed Tony.

"I don't know why he has such a problem with us," pointed out Mac.

"Oh, don't take it personally, he has a problem with everyone!" chirped in Mark, which caused Tony to nearly spray the coffee from his mouth whilst choking for air.

The three of them laughed again before Mac spoke up "You know, I have an idea concerning our friends across town. You know they are going to run us off the park by throwing everything they have against us with the view to crushing us into submission" he continued.

"That's a pretty fair assessment, if I know our esteemed colleague, as well as I think I do," added Tony.

"Well, as you're probably aware, they will be expecting us to do the norm and absorb the pressure and hope to take them on the counter. But I thought that maybe we could utilise the rehabilitated twosome and give them something a little unexpected later in the game."

"Go on," said Tony.

"For me," continued Ma, "this tactic is all about morale and raising the self belief of your team around you. You know there is nothing better than to see a group of men perform an act that is way above and beyond their expectations, because once they've achieved it, they will do it again. Whilst in Special Forces, we were tasked with recovering a peace keeping medic that had been taken hostage by a breakaway gang of unsavoury thugs, looking for political gain for what was a pretty pointless cause. Anyway, with no more than eight men and after carrying out 3 days of intensive covert ops, we launched an attack to both neutralise the aggressors and recover the aid worker but during the raid, the gang were fortunate enough to increase in numbers as a neighbouring gang joined them to assist," continued Mac and looked up.

Both Tony and Mark where engrossed in the story and hanging on to Mac's every last word. Smirking he continued "We were already outnumbered, so with the increase in numbers the task in hand was beginning to look like a possible retreat on our part and that was something we never took lightly. We were low on ammo and equipment as our army Bergens had been lost whilst withdrawing and we were really starting to feel the pressure of being surrounded. Well, that was until one of our men stepped up to the plate and threw caution to the wind by running through a patch of open ground and straight towards enemy fire. Somehow, and I have no idea to this day how he did it, he managed to run through the line of men and out the other side where he managed to access some of our Bergens. Grabbing essential equipment, he spun on his heels and ran back through the line of purblind, armed to the teeth gang members and back to his unit. Surprisingly, he managed to return completely unscathed. It was as if it happened in slow motion and I don't know who was more surprised; them or us? Anyway, not only did he manage to supply enough equipment for us to break through their ranks but, and more importantly, his actions had the instant effect of quadrupling morale. Before we knew it we had the upper hand and were soon on the way to finishing the job we had come to do," said Mac smirking to himself. "And that, my friends, is how you get the job done; by inspiring your team mates well beyond the limits of their comfort zones with an 'off the charts' game plan on the field of play that is so dramatic that your opposition just won't know what hit them."

All three men were silent for a time before Tony responded "But why the gruesome twosome?"

Mark now jumped in "Because they are about ready for action. These past couple of months I have chucked just about everything at them to try and break them into submission and, surprisingly, they have risen to the challenge and in some cases well beyond... and for what? To stay at Handley Park Rangers? Of course not! No, they came alive when someone climbed in their face and told them straight, and in no uncertain terms, where they stand with them. But in doing so, it also demonstrated that someone cared enough about them to fight for them and do you know what? It was the caring about them that finally broke them and had them sobbing like babies. Those two lads have really been through the mill," he continued. "It gave them value and worth and they just lapped it up and have both grown remarkably as young men. If we can tap into their strengths, whilst maintaining a discipline, then we could well be sitting on some secret weapons that can come off the subs bench and change things up dramatically."

"And you go along with all this?" said Tony now turning to Mac. "Even with Darren, who you described as 9 out of 10 on the punchometer?"

"I know," commented a rather surprised Mac" but from what Mark tells me, he has gone to the root cause with these two boys and believes that they are almost unrecognizable from the two lads who met with him early one morning back in March."

"So we have ourselves a couple of super subs," said Tony nodding his head slowly as if starting to believe the concept.

"I believe we do," added Mac.

"Well, if we are going to face the giants across the border, we'd better hear some more of this crazy plan of yours," suggested Tony.

"Yeah, especially the bit about behind enemy lines!" remarked Mark trying to pull Mac's leg.

32

Here we go! Battle stations....

"If the good book states that a quiet word turns away wrath, then why did you have to go out of your way to antagonize our frenemy across the border?" expressed Mark to Tony as they journeyed north across the counties.

"I don't believe I put anyone's nose out of joint," conceded Tony. "In fact, I thought I'd demonstrated the height of diplomacy with my clipped responses, thus preventing things from getting personal."

"So telling their head coach that his management style was antiquated and that it was a pity Noah was busy with his Ark as he could have done a better job at managing his team, had no vitriol undertones?" concluded Mac cutting in.

"Well, I guess if you put it like that, well then maybe I could have toned things down a tad," considered Tony.

"You think!" insisted Mac with a hint of sarcasm.

Tony shrugged whilst slightly twisting his neck, kind of implying that sometimes you just have to roll with the punches. Quickly changing the subject Tony asked "More importantly, do you think our secret weapons are ready for tonight?"

"Not altogether sure about where their heads are at but they are certainly at peak fitness, " offered Mac.

"What about you Mark? What do you think?" asked Tony.

"Well hopefully it is not too soon as they've both travelled an unexpected path of rehabilitation but, you know what? When is the right time? And as they say 'if it is to be, it's up to me'. Well then, why not now?" claimed Mark

"Don't you think it's a bit risky, considering we are in an FA Cup tie with a team that are keen to wipe us off the face of the Ordnance survey map?" reminded Mac.

Tony rubbed the top of his legs "D'you know what? No I don't, so if during the game the opportunity arises, I think we should go for it" decided Tony. He continued "We desperately need some sort of a card up our sleeve if we are going to cause an upset and our reformed boys just might be that solution we need right now."

Big Mac knew Tony was right as this game would be by far the most physically challenging yet. Don't get me wrong, their opponents weren't exactly in form or flying high in their Division 1 league. No, the problem with this encounter was that Handley Park were receiving unmerited media attention due to their own recent successes and as far as their opponents were concerned, this was not acceptable as they were supposed to be the team in the limelight, not some bunch of part timers from a sleepy little market town. Mac pulled into the car park adjacent to their opponents towering stadium with wrap around polished granite tile. A club superstore depicting images of the club's rising stars sat just by the hospitality entrance and furthest away, to the north stand entrance, sat a trendy hotel lobby overlooking a cluster of retail outlet stores. "Pretty impressive wouldn't you say? Anyone fancy a coffee" asked Mac.

"No, not now," asserted Tony. "Let's get inside and settle the lads' nerves."

The squad had congregated and were sitting on the bonnets of their estate cars and car derived vans and seemed somewhat subdued. You see, they had allowed themselves to become intimidated by their surroundings, well, all except Clay as it did not seem to bother Clay where or who he played. Without hesitating, Tony walked right into the centre of their conversation and boldly told them to stop it.

"Stop what?" asked Sam.

"You know what! I want to stop the rot right now of you lot talking yourself into feeling inferior just because of some fancy palace in front of you. Yes, it may house a few more seats than ours (Mac whispered in Mark's ear "Try 29544 more seats") but remember they have far more to lose than us. Either way, I'm not interested in them. No, I'm interested in you lot; our motley crew. You see, we," Tony says whilst fanning his arm in the direction of Mac and Mark "we believe in you 110%. In fact, right at this moment we would pitch you against any team in the land and expect you to give them a run for their money! That is how much we believe in you. But you have to reciprocate by believing the same yourselves and not allowing fancy stadiums or flashy cars to unnerve you," Tony continued. "So, this afternoon, my friends, it's your hosts who have the displeasure of your company and I want every one of them to rue the day they were faced with you. Now, do I need to continue blowing smoke towards your nether regions or shall we go and prepare for battle?" and with that he spun on his heels and headed in the direction of the stadium entrance.

"I think he might have a point or two there," remarked Mark. "Anyone care to join us?" and with that the lads hoisted their kits bags and fell in line.

"No one's up for a quick coffee then?" asked Big Mac but his words just fell on deaf ears as the lads filed through the doors and were gone.

The match itself was what you would describe as somewhat physical, with plenty of strong armed tactics courtesy of Handley Park's hosts. As, after all, it is a contact sport. Throughout, most tackles comprised of two hits; the hosts engaging with a Handley Park player by hitting them with all they had, followed by the aforementioned HPR player hitting the floor. With that said, Handley Park managed to retain not only its shape but more importantly its discipline, by not reacting in any way to the adopted dirty tactics. Instead, they chose to dust themselves off and get back on with the game.

However, deep into the second half, the squads' discipline was tested beyond restraint when Clay, having gauged his usual quarter back stance in preparation to launch one of his clinical throws, found himself brutally caught on his forearm with a high boot from an off-side winger. Of course it was meant as an act of underhand play which left the Handley Park squad losing their heads, momentarily and engaging in a way that left the referee with no alternative but to intervene with yellow cards galore. In fact, it transpired that Handley Park's left winger received a second yellow and had to leave the field of play. Now, not only were HPR down to 10 men but their unbeaten keeper had to be replaced in order to receive medical attention. To any outsider, it would appear that Handley Park's number was up as there was still half an hour of play left, they were a man down and their star goalkeeper was off injured. But as far as Tony, Mac and Mark were concerned it was their opportunity.

"Cometh the hour, cometh the man. Or men in our case," dared Tony as he turned to Mac. "Make the changes Mac and let's implement fully your shock and awe tactic we spoke about."

For a minute Mac stopped in his tracks before replying "You don't mean the story about recovering a medic?"

"Yes, the very one," challenged Tony.

"But I was only reminiscing about the good old days," groaned Mac.

"You may have been," stated Tony" but I want us to go all out for the win and see if somehow we can recover this game. And not just for Clay, but for all of us as I'm sick of our lads being used for target practice. To be honest, if I see one more dirty tackle, I'm going out there to sort things out myself."

Mac nodded and was soon on his toes organising the necessary changes. Whilst Darren and Frank stripped, Mac stood between them, far too close for comfort. He explained just how important this game was to them all and how he expected them to hit the ground running the moment they were on the pitch. Nothing was left to chance, Darren was told to keep goal as if his life depended on it and Frank was to take the game to the enemy.

"No fear guys," were Mac's last words as a tactical substitution was made to accommodate Frank. The game quickly recommenced and within no time, the home side were on top, smelling blood and looking to strike first. But somehow the Handley Park defence held firm, especially with the rejuvenated Darren in goal, directing and encouraging his teammates. He managed to really own his space and instil some much needed confidence at the back, which in turn allowed the back four to soak up the pressure really well. Until eventually, with a little over 5 minutes of play left, Frank, at the heels of an opponent, pickpocketed him with some fancy footwork and was soon on his toes exiting their half of the field, for the first time in half an hour. He was soon surrounded by a swarm of midfielders keen to stop him in his tracks. But, not deterred, he continued firstly by weaving in and out of two midfielders before completing a sharp angled one-two with Graham. He then shimmied his way around a central defender and was no more than 10 yards from the penalty area when one of the dirtiest hackers on the field steamed in with a flying tackle. Some 6 months prior, Frank would have been more than proud of such a reckless attempt to tackle, but not this newly reformed character. No, somehow he managed to stay on his feet, move the ball forward for him to run onto and skip over the flying legs of his opponent. Now finding himself face-to-face with a rather shocked goalie, he prepared to rocket the ball beyond the keeper's reach. But at the last minute, he passed the ball instinctively across the face of goal and into the running path of Sam, who had just covered best part of 50 yards to keep up. Without a second thought, Sam volleyed the ball so sweetly that it hit the back of the net before anyone had a chance to react. Silence descended throughout the stadium. It was as if no one could register what had just happened. As for Handley Park, instead of bundling Sam, they all ran to the dugout, celebrating in unison with the entire squad.

After that, Handley Park pretty much parked their defensive bus, soaking up any attempts of pressure and running down the clock in anticipation of the final whistle. At the whistle any attempts of sportsmanlike handshakes by Handley Park proved futile not only amongst the players but the management teams as well. Later on in the dressing room, the jubilation was infectious for as far as Tony, Mac and Mark were concerned, each player had battled hard for their space and overcome their Goliath. They commended each man for their efforts especially Frank and Darren who had turned the game on its head with sterling performances. Finally everyone settled down and Tony spoke "I just want you all to remember this game today guys. Remember what we said about giving anyone a run for their money. Because gentleman, we are by no means finished with this cup run yet. In fact, we're just getting warmed up. Now, who fancies a little shindig courtesy of our friendly Italian restaurateur?"

33

The Infamous Mug

Tony, Big Mac and Mark were on tender hooks. It was D-day as Kieran and Graham were about to meet for the first time in almost three years; and a lot of water had gone under that bridge since then. The guys had arranged for them to meet in Nigel's old office so they were busy doing their best to tidy whilst Tony added some "homey touches" as he liked to call it. Big Mac and Mark were bickering over by the old Butler sink as Mark threatened, yet again, to wash or, even better still, destroy Big Mac's cherished mug. The usual threats of violence by Mac ensued, resulting in Mark stating that he would rinse the mug with washing up liquid if he came one step closer. You see, Mac had carried that same old mug with him for the last two decades and had never once washed it, believing that the flavour not only stemmed from the tea bag but more importantly from the specially infused flavours and stains historically left behind in the bottom of the mug. As far as Mark was concerned, the mug was a public health risk and should have been donated to science years ago as it probably contained undiscovered forms of bacteria. Truth be told, the banter was no more than a futile attempt to distract them from what was likely to be a possible showdown or a hopeful reunion; either way today was going to be a challenge. A decision was made that if Graham could not come to terms with Kieran's involvement, then they would all walk away from what was their only potential benefactor; which was why they were all so keen for the meeting to bode well. It was agreed that Mark would mediate and Big Mac would be around as moral support for Graham.

Just before midday, Tony was slung out and told to take his 'homey touches' with him, along with Mac's diseased mug. Now alone, Mac could sense that Mark was feeling the strain as he watched him mimic the introductory moves of a conductor about to address his orchestra in an attempt to steady his nerves. He watched him focus on his breathing and noticed how one minute he was seated and the next he was pacing the room. Mac remained quiet and slightly out of the way, which was just how he liked it. They did not have to wait long before Graham arrived looking like a bag of nerves himself, closely followed by Kieran. Mark, now the perfect host, guided them to some comfy chairs, offered a hot beverage and then sat down next to them, remaining reticent in the hope that the ice would soon break.

Surprisingly, it was Graham who spoke first. "Kieran, I guess I thought I would never see this day but I'm genuinely glad to meet you. If I'm honest, life's been a bit of a rollercoaster for me over the last few years and, at times, I've been best described as a very "Angry Elf". Not content with that accolade, I've added several pity parties in my honour but, truth be told, I'm tired and done with all that now. Yes, of course I would like to, in fact I need to, fill in the blanks surrounding the first time we met but more importantly, right now, I'd like nothing better than for us to build some sort of a bridge and see if we can get over what has gone before together. You up for it?"

Kieran blinked in disbelief, absolutely flabbergasted by Graham's opening gambit which kind of took him off guard. But before he had a chance to weigh up or respond, a loud sobbing noise resonated throughout the room, which left Kieran and Graham looking at each other quizzically before turning their attention to their old friend and mentor. Poor Mark; the strong one, the go-to man in a crisis. The one who allegedly had all his ducks in a row, was so overcome with emotion that he was unable to keep himself in check. In fact both men had to delay their catch up in order to attend to Mark who just was not able to turn off the waterworks. Mark, now rambling in between sobs tried to explain how embarrassed he was and that his behaviour was not befitting a   professional of his stature. Either way, the tears continued along with mucus that was now combining as it exited every orifice available on his face. Eventually, Mark was inter-rupted mid-sentence by a gentle tap on the shoulder as Big Mac stepped in and gently guided him from his seat and led him outside and down the corridor towards the toilets and makeshift Spa. Mark popped to the loo for a minute to gather his thoughts whilst Mac went in search of Tony. Whilst Mark was taking a moment, Mac quickly briefed Tony stating that things were looking pretty good between Graham and Kieran whilst at the same time discreetly mentioning that he should go easy on Mark as he'd had a bit of an unexpected meltdown whilst with them. Tony asked where Mark was and how was he doing and Mac responded by saying he'd taken a minute on his own and would join them shortly.

Mark joined them just as Tony was stepping into the hot tub and looking up at Mark with utmost sincerity, stated that he was relieved to hear, at long last, that, perhaps, Mark was not a machine and maybe human after all. "That's the ticket," thought Big Mac to himself, "nice and easy does it Tony, let's keep the conversation light and not too deep."

Mark forced a grin. Tony, now easing his way into the effervescent water continued "I guess now we're going to have to change your nickname from the running to the crying man" and with that he ducked his head under the water to enjoy the full force of the jets.

Mark winced slightly, aghast at Tony's out of line comment. He felt the surge of rage within him but managed to steady the ship knowing that a calculated response here would be far better than a quick reaction. He turned to Big Mac just in time to see not only Mac's jaw drop but that cherished, tea stained mug of his, drop from his hand in what appeared slow motion and tumble to the floor smashing into smithereens. Big Mac and Mark now staring, wide eyed, initially at the mess on the floor, looked at each other in disbelief thinking to themselves "Did he really just say that?" And as their minds registered what had just happened Tony, totally oblivious, resurfaced shouting over the noise of the jets that they should join him as it was so relaxing. They seemed preoccupied so he shouted again "Come on, are you coming in then?" and before they could respond he was gone again below the surface. Mark and Mac now crouching down to pick up pieces of the mug began shaking their heads and when Mac pushed Mark on the shoulder they started laughing a little. Mark pushed him back and before long they had both lost the plot and were laughing uncontrollably on the floor.

Tony's head popped above the bubbles, looking at them both on the floor which made them laugh even more and had them both holding their sides. He sat bolt upright and asked "What on earth is going on with you two?" but his question just had them in fits of laughter again as they were no longer able to control themselves, so Tony just stood up and walked past them both shaking his head whilst saying under his breath "I don't know about those two. I really do worry about them at times." And with that, he left to go and change.

34

The Ageing Warrior

John Vossa sat in his director's chair, in his recently refurbished office being blasted with copious amounts of cool air conditioning. He enjoyed the high life and the luxuries it rewarded, but boy was he bored and it wasn't even mid morning. Elevenses was at least an hour away, which would help kill some time, but he couldn't just eat his way through his boredom, especially as he believed he still had one more fight left in him when it came to his beloved game of football. The thing that was really playing on John's mind was an old school friend of his, who ran a church on the outskirts of town, had quoted this bible verse from Ecclesiastes 1 about a chap he said was the first ever billionaire and how he saw many similarities between him and John. He referred to everything as being like smoke in the wind and what really annoyed him was that this mate of his was right. It was as if everything had lost its flavour right now, but there was no need to shove it in John's face; his mate was lucky he didn't get a punch on the nose.

You see, to all intents and purposes he had it all; a polished career as a professional footballer that spanned almost two decades, plenty of silverware locked away in his own private trophy cabinet, a good few quid in the bank, a beautiful wife with 3 adorable children; oh and 2 businesses including a thriving car dealership along with a solid investment portfolio to boot. Problem was, since leaving his beloved Prem' club that he had served both as man and boy, he felt totally lost and empty inside. You see, the camaraderie of his teammates along with the banter and a host of faceless fans that had chanted his name for so many years, had filled the void in his life for such a long time and had given him the significance and worth that he had so desperately longed for as a young lad. John's wife Becky, his childhood sweetheart, knew him inside and out; she knew he was lost. It was as if he was floating out to sea aimlessly on a makeshift raft and with no sense of direction. Problem with that was that she knew he was unreachable right now and she found it so upsetting to sit on the sidelines of his life, watching the man she loved so much being tossed around in a storm.

The only ray of hope that Becky could see on the horizon was John's budding friendship with his cherished car valeter, Clay Jackson. For some unknown reason, John had been drawn to Clay, pretty much from the moment he joined his prestige used car showroom. In fact, because of this unexpected bromance, a few noses had been put out of joint especially John's general manager Stan Harvey. Now Stan loved the idea of working for an ex-premiership football star, for as far as he was concerned, it made him windswept and interesting, especially in front of the ladies; therefore he wasn't about to let his meal ticket be led astray by some backward Yank. He just needed the opportunity to muddy the waters of that relationship a little and make sure John knew what a star he had in "Stan the man".

The following Friday, Clay arranged to meet with Tony at the new executive used car dealership he'd recently commenced employment with. They grabbed a bite at Giovanni's in town and spoke about Clay's progress in the squad, how he was getting on with some of the other players and after that, they just hung out as Tony liked Clay's company. He was wholesome and spoke with such wisdom on most subjects, plus Tony believed this lad was packed full of natural gifts and talents that were waiting to be unearthed. They made their way back to the dealership and as Tony turned in to the customer parking area, he pulled alongside a rather desirable Porsche 911. Its occupant, John Vossa, had just climbed out and in recognising Clay walked over to them. John knelt down by Clay's window and began thanking him for the excellent valet he had just completed on his mate's car and by way of an appreciation a small gift had been left inside for him. Clay did his usual play it down response and covered his mild embarrassment by introducing Tony. The two men exchanged the normal surface small talk pleasantries and Tony was about to sign off by bidding both Clay and John farewell but he had this overwhelming notion that maybe he should engage a little longer with this John character.

He climbed out of his not so desirable looking car and continued his conversation some more with John. Clay could sense that Tony was up to something so left the men together talking. They spoke about cars, of course, and soon found themselves talking in depth about football. Tony shared a little about Handley Park Rangers before John finally succumbed to Tony's prompts and soon began sharing about his career in football. Tony soon realised there was nothing hubristic about this guy as he was, from what he could tell, the real deal and he had the accolades to prove it. Interestingly though, was that Tony could sense an almost melancholic tone to John's voice as if something was not quite right or maybe amiss. Sure this "death by marble" dealership he was standing in was impressive; especially if you were looking to part with a few quid, but Tony could tell that this guy needed a little more in his life right now than a need for speed.

Their conversation was somewhat interrupted by a rather pompous looking man who was keen to get John's full attention and for no apparent reason other than the fact that he liked the sound of his own voice. This chap turned out to be John's general manager, Stan who was keen to talk about one of his favourite subjects: namely himself and it was not difficult, for any outsider, to see just how unimpressed John was with this rather annoying, sycophant little man. Just as Stan was about to launch full throttle into how amazing he was at his role as GM, he was rather rudely interrupted by one of his minions stating that the usual lunch time tyre kicker (time waster) was out walking amongst the cars on the lot and should he think about moving him on as he had better things to do with his time than to engage with the likes of him. From John's point of view, the whole conversation was tiresome to say the least, not though for Tony as the art of selling (or lack of in this case) was what always gave him that fire in the belly; which of course was no great surprise for a man who sold motivation and sales training for a living. The minion of a sales executive was about to go out and confront the 'perp', accusing him of loitering with intent; the crime being that he was cluttering the place up. Cue Tony, as he could take it no more, so he blocked the way of the minion suggesting that maybe he could help out. The spotlight immediately turned on Tony as the three men shifted their gaze in his direction. Both Stan and his minion, looking somewhat perturbed, suggested to John that maybe this guy with him should butt out, which of course intrigued the life out of the whole situation as far as John was concerned.

Tony, reading the situation well, knew now that he had John's full attention so chose to ignore the protests of John's foot soldiers and rounded on him with the express aim of a wager. They looked at each other intently for a time before John spoke "So, what's on your mind Tony?"

In replying, Tony suggested the same - that maybe there was something on John's mind too. They were both in the zone now, knowing that there was some kind of challenge in the air. Tony turned slightly and pointing said to John "That chap out there, you know the supposed tyre kicker? What if I were to sell him one of your luxury cars?"

John replied "Now why would you want to go and do that Tony? You looking for some commission?"

Tony laughed and said "I might be! Especially with the prices you charge! But no, I'm more interested in a little wager with you."

John replied "Ahhhhh there it is. Looking for some kind of a job, are we?"

Tony chuckled to himself and replied "Funnily enough, I was looking for some kind of job for you"

John's turn "For me? Now, what can you do for me?"

Tony came back, "Well, for starters, I can make you some money by selling that supposed time waster out there a car and to boot I will even tell you right now what car he is going to buy."

John came back again "And in return?"

Tony replied "Well, you dust off those old boots of yours and come and help out at Handley Park Rangers."

Replying, John said "And why would I want to do that?"

Tony again "Because, John, you're bored out of your brains and are desperate to get your teeth back into something."

John went to speak but could not and found himself motionless as his head whirled and his heart started racing. He thought to himself 'Who does this guy think he is? Giving it the "Charlie Big Potato" about selling one of my luxury cars to a tyre kicker and then expecting me to lower myself and go and play for a tin pot non-league football team?'

He looked around for help, thinking that maybe he could side step this lunatic by chastising Stan about something or other, but they were long gone, probably pushing paperwork somewhere trying to look busy and important. He looked again at Tony expecting to find a cold, challenging poker face but instead he was met with a face that shone with true compassion. John impulsively kissed his teeth and narrowed his gaze as he tried to think up some sort of comeback but he had nothing. So instead, to buy himself some time, he suggested to Tony "So, show me what you've got," as he nodded in the direction of the car lot. As Tony walked off, he called after him "So what car will he be buying bigshot?" but Tony just kept walking stating that the piece of paper on the coffee table in front of him would provide the answer. John bent down and grabbed the folded piece of paper and was about to open it when Clay walked past. He called out to him and said "Who does this Tony guy think he is?"
Clay replied "What do you mean?"
"Well, he's kind of getting under my skin, making out he's some kind of cream of the crop salesman whilst telling me I should help out at Handley Park."
Clay replied "So how has he done that?"
John stated "Well, we were talking about some sort of wager."
Clay replied "Which was?"
John continued "That if he sold one of my cars to the tyre kicker outside, then in return I would dust off my boots and join Handley Park Rangers."
"He stated that did he? He must want you badly," responded

Clay.

"I'm not even going to give it a thought. I've seen that time waster here so many times over the months, so he might be able to sell snow to Eskimos, but he won't be selling one of my cars today. What do you think Clay?" prompted John.

Clay looked at John sincerely "You really want to know what I think, coming from a man that supposedly has everything?"

"Just tell me what you think" pleaded John hastily.

"I think you should dust your boots off John because that man means business and when he wants something or someone then he goes after them 110%."

John replied "I just thought he wanted a job or to earn himself a bit of commission but going back to football and a non-league club at that, would make me a laughing stock! No, that is a bridge too far for me. What does he even do for a living anyway?"

"He motivates and inspires people to be the best person they can be."

"What at playing football or selling cars?" suggested John sarcastically.

"No, at doing life" declared Clay.

"Do you think he will sell that guy a car?" added John.

"No, I know he will sell that man a car" confided Clay.

"But I don't need help from someone regarding playing football again," interjected John.

"I know," stated Clay "but you do need help seeing beyond football and into the future as all this stuff around you is not doing it for you, is it?"

Just then Stan came to join them to make sure he was not missing out on anything, which coincided with Tony entering the warmth of the showroom with his customer. Stan looked smugly at Tony, expecting to be asked for some sort of help to bail him out of an embarrassing situation, but instead Tony handed, on a plate I might add, his customer asking Stan if he would not mind completing the paperwork and securing a rather large deposit for the green Morgan sitting on the front row. Jaws dropped from both John and Stan as Tony thanked the customer for his time and his business, stating that he was in good hands with Stan. Tony now turned to John, who thought to himself 'here we go, to the victor go the spoils," but instead Tony just stated;

"It was great to meet with you John and I do hope we meet again. Oh and Clay, I'll see you at training tonight," and with that Tony left but not without John finally asking "How on earth did you know what car that guy was going to buy?"

"Oh that was easy," answered Tony. "I just chose the car he kept avoiding" and with that he was gone.

For a minute John was speechless as he wasn't used to being out manoeuvred but, truth be told, he was beginning to like the tension he was sensing as it made him feel quite alive inside rather than his usual monotone self. He looked over to Stan now sitting with the customer. As he listened yet again to the dulcet tones of his sycophant general manager boring the customer about his role as GM of such a prestigious car franchise he thought to himself 'maybe it is time, after all, to dust those boots off for one last showdown' and laughed to himself. 'Now, where is that Clay Jackson?' John thought. He didn't mention he played at Handley Park Rangers!' and with that, he went in pursuit of him.

35

A reluctant Addition to the Squad

"D'you know I've just passed two brass monkeys in the street crying due to the cold out there!" declared Frank who did have a tendency to over exaggerate at the best of times. "I know what you mean," bemoaned his "wingman" Darren, "you'd have thought 'the running man" ' would have given us a night off from training tonight, what with all of this crazy weather at the moment. Half the time I have no idea what to wear," he remarked to no one in particular.

"Listen you two! If it ain't raining, it ain't training as my old captain used to say!" challenged Mac "so let's put a lid on the moaning by closing that hole under our noses and focusing on what our esteemed colleague has to say."

But Mac's chastised remarks fell on deaf ears as the distinct roar of a Supercar sparked interest as it entered the club's dimly lit car park, pulling alongside the patched up, meshed security fence. Mac, now joined by Mark and the rest of the team congregated by the fence as they wondered who on earth the occupants could be.

"It's probably an old flame of mine looking for a second chance," remarked Frank.

"No I reckon it's my agent who's come to discuss rumours of a big move for me!" added Darren.

"Yeah right oh! You wish," blurted out one of the players.

But to everyone's surprise, a familiar face appeared from behind the passenger gull wing door in the form of Clay as he struggled to pull himself out of his Recaro sports seat. He waved to his team mates as he waited patiently for the driver to emerge. The driver, for some reason, appeared somewhat reluctant to step out of his car but after a little persuasion from Clay, none other than John Vossa, ex-Premier League legend appeared. Utter silence descended from both sides of the crooked fence. Big Mac stared at Mark in disbelief and simply stated, "Is that who I think it is?"

But before anyone had a chance to respond, Tony joined the foray and interjected by confirming that yes it was him and that yes he'd kindly offered to join the fray, for a period of time.

"He doesn't look overly keen to be here," commented one of the lads.

"Ah looks can be deceiving," chipped in Tony, "he just needs a little time to adjust to his new surroundings that's all."

As Tony spun on his heels, Mac, closely followed by Mark blocked his way hoping to have a quick word.

"What's on your mind Mac" asked Tony a little too nonchalantly.

"I think you know what's on mine, no our minds!" stressed Mac. Pointing in the direction of John and Clay he continued, "What's he doing here?"

"Look, it's nothing sinister. To be honest I thought I'd mentioned it earlier. Anyway, I happened to bump into John whilst lunching with Clay the other week and we kind of hit it off" advised Tony.

"Oh that's nice," chipped in Mac rather flippantly. "And what did we talk about?"

"Alright Mac calm down," stated Tony. "All we did was talk a little about football."

"And from a cozy chat we now have an ex- Prem star popping along for a light training session?" quizzed Mac.

"Oh there was a bit more to it as his annoying manager kept interrupting. Which kind of got my goat a little. And well I..." ruminated Tony.

"Well I errr what?" challenged Mac.

"It was something and nothing really. I just happened to notice a customer of theirs being ignored as the sales staff had perceived him as no more than a tyre kicker so I suggested that maybe I could step in and help out!" replied Tony.

"Sounds very admirable of you but still doesn't explain why he's here!" prompted Mac. "Well, my offer of help was kind of misconstrued as a wager I believe!" advised Tony. "Oh. How so?" baited Mac.

"Somehow John was under the impression that if I managed to sell his luxury car on the lot, that in return he could dust off his boots and come and help us out here at the club!" explained Tony.

"Now I wonder how he came to that conclusion!" goaded Mac.

Tony, choosing to ignore Mac' digs continued. "Thing is guys, from the small amount of time I spent with him, I could sense an almost civil war raging within him as he seemed to be struggling with coming to terms with his life outside of football. You know, for someone who allegedly has everything there seems to be a profound emptiness in his eyes. Anyway, once I'd established a need I felt duty bound to lay down the gauntlet and challenge him. Interestingly enough though, once I'd laid down the gauntlet he seemed to come alive and went on to demonstrate that he still has plenty of fire left in the belly." explained Tony whilst shrugging his shoulders as an act of "what's a man to do?"

"You're a one, you really are! Why can't you just meet new people with a simple hello and goodbye?" declared Mac.

"Always been the same I guess," conceded Tony. "If I see an opportunity, then I'm right in there."

"I know," smiled Mac. "That's what makes you, you is all!"

"Either way though, he's not too chuffed about being here is he?" observed Mac. "You're not wrong there," chipped in Mark.

"And that, my dear friends, is why you guys need to sprinkle your touch of magic and bring him into the fold," coaxed Tony.

"And how d'you propose we do that?" retorted both men.

"Simple!" implied Tony. " John will soon recognise that this squad of ours is playing well above their remit of ability. He'll be intrigued and want to know more. He'll want to know why a group of blokes stick together when there is no money passing hands. He'll want to know why we're still together whilst those around are mocking us as no more than a laughing stock. Once he sees all of that, he'll either run a mile or recognise the opportunity and embrace it. That's all we can do but I'll tell you now, having seen the look in his eyes, my money's on him rolling his sleeves up! And, if I'm right we may just have elevated this young team to another level of ability and self belief. What d'you think?" asked Tony.

"I'm not sure," declared Mac. "Could be too much of a risk."

"I know," chipped in Mark "but what if it pays off? Either way, it'll certainly cause a stir further up the food chain of the footballing elite!"

"Could be fun!" laughed Mark.

"Yes it could be fun!" shouted Tony.

Mac sighed in his usual manner and laughed to himself before declaring, "Yes it could be fun!"

And with that the coaches headed out to meet a rather nervous looking John Vossa to welcome him to the team.

36

A Blank Canvas

Giovanni kindly handed over the reins of his authentic Italian cafe to the players and staff of Handley Park Rangers so that they could meet and discuss if the club had any chance of securing a future, given the financial predicament or 'account's black hole' as they liked to call it. You see, the club was in a mess and on the verge of collapse. Not everyone knew but those who did, were aware of the battle on their hands. Copious amounts of Caffe Borghetti were served along with Giovanni's renowned delicious mushroom shaped Baba cakes. In all, there were just over thirty people in attendance, which included the full backroom management committee, an accounts administrator, the last of the dwindling number of over vexed volunteers and the full squad along with Tony, Mac and Mark. The meeting got off to a rocky start with both the vice chairman and accounts administrator announcing that they would be standing down from their posts forthwith. Which, of course, could have easily triggered a domino effect had it not been for the cafe owner and lifelong fan of Handley Park Rangers; Giovanni. He, of all people, was the one who stepped in and shared passionately the support and belief he had in the new management team; their selfless commitment to seeing the job through by leading the club back on to a safer, more secure, even keel.

After a rather emotional, if not lengthy, drawn out plea by Giovanni, Tony stood and took centre stage. He thanked the management committee for their sterling efforts over the last couple of years and met both resignations with compassion and understanding. He then followed up by commending the volunteers that had religiously served the club, both in the good and bad time,s before finally going on to share how he believed that the future of the club was now in all of their hands. Overall control of the club, thanks to Kieran and his legal team, could eventually pass to the good people of this town once they had dealt with the legalities surrounding the disappearance of Nigel Hawkson. (he left the bit out about being unable to find Nigel but that would be a discussion for another time). He purposefully kept the meeting short and as upbeat as possible as he wanted to spend more time with the players and help focus them.

In all there were now 19 registered players available to the club. So far, they had weathered the storm of being downtrodden and bullied by former manager, Mike Phillips and his recently reformed son Darren. Somehow the club had managed to avoid the relegation trap door and remain in their tier 8, East Midlands league. Plus, and not forgetting the fact, for best part of a year, none of the players had received any form of payment for play rendered. But since the appointment of Tony, along with the revival of Big Mac and the addition of Mark the "running man", the squad had managed, unbelievably, to keep its shape and unity. With the new season now 3 months in, Handley Park were sitting 4th in their league and had even managed to remain in the FA Cup competition. In truth bar, a couple of epic battles, it was more by good fortune than judgement but either way they were still in the tournament. Clay Jackson was now the club's official 1st choice keeper; Darren Phillips, after discovering that he possessed a blistering pace to get him out of trouble when necessary, was fast becoming the go-to man for defensive duties whilst Frank Malone, under the watchful eye of ex-pro John Vossa, was the engine room of the midfield. Finally the two rookies; Graham Krusher and Sam Ryan were the potential goal machines that were yet to hit form but showed real promise that was supported with a strenuous work ethic.

Throughout the summer, the management team had worked tirelessly with the squad, adding new players and releasing players that did not quite match the profile they were looking for. You see, the team needed men that were both teachable and pliable to new ideas and different ways of thinking. Couple that with an insatiable desire to train and train hard and you have the beginnings of a winning formula. All of this was sold on the basis of looking at the bigger picture. It had to be; purely for the very reason that on paper the club was a laughing stock with no money available, a handful of fans and volunteers and a ground that was in dire need of refurbishment. With all of that aside, somehow, the management team had managed to instil the beginnings of some self belief, not only in the players as individuals, but also as a team.

Tony felt the time was right to move the players on a level by challenging their goal orientation. So now with the players all grouped together, pretty chilled out and comfortable with those around them and their surroundings, he began by asking them if they set themselves goals or targets. The usual suspects responded, those who were eager to please or be heard, but Tony was not satisfied with leaving it at that. No, he wanted to ruffle the feathers of those avoiding eye contact or those that were starting to look bored as their eyes glazed over. So out he came with it

"Let's have some of your goals, dreams, desires! I want to know what floats your boat," as he liked to word it.

The signs of discomfort were starting to show, especially with John Vossa who was still busy trying to find his feet at the club. Tony, not one to be deterred, pushed on.

"So," only the sound of imaginary tumbleweeds rushing between the cafe walk ways broke the quietness. "Nothing, so nobody has any goals or objectives they would like to reach and achieve?"

Big Mac went to cut in but Tony's stern look made him reconsider. Silence continued for what seemed like an age before John piped in "What's all this got to do with us kicking a ball?" which of course lightened the mood a little and gave the team confidence in numbers to create slight murmurs of displeasure, which in truth was exactly what Tony wanted, especially from John.

Tony responded "Good question John. So what are your future goals and dreams for the next few years?"

John, now begrudgingly in the spotlight, chose to make light of the situation by explaining how wasn't it Tony who only recently described John as the man who had everything to which Tony responded with

"But did I John or did I merely point out that maybe you thought you had everything in life that you needed?"

That got John's mind reeling, preparing for a comeback that would blow Tony out of the water.

'How dare he?' John thought to himself. 'Who does this guy think he is?'

But for John there would be no let up as Tony, reading the signs of fight or flight flowing through John's mind, chose to go a step further by moving uncomfortably closer to John and invading his personal bubble of privacy. For John that was a bridge too far. He turned to face Tony, ready to launch an avalanche of abuse and profanity, but when he looked into Tony' eyes, all he could see was total compassion and an inner strength that could not be breached. He went to gesticulate as a means to offer something in retaliation, but he had nothing in him. He tried to rack his brains, looking for a counter that would provide some form of self preservation and a swift exit, but nothing came. It was as if he was rooted to the spot and with no means of defence. He felt sure that any minute now Tony would come in for the kill and offer John's scalp up as a sacrifice, proving to the other players who the daddy or alpha male was. But instead it was Tony who was moved to tears as he turned to the other players and wept openly in front of them. Finally he spoke. "You know guys, I love you all like brothers and I genuinely want the best for you. What I am trying to do here is to get you to look beyond football and to not accept second best."

Tony went on to share a story about his life and how he had been brought to a place of feeling uncomfortable about how he viewed his life. Finally, after a period of soul searching, he stumbled across some infinite wisdom that had helped him create a lifelong plan for his life. It was simplistic in its form and yet had given him the inner strength and belief to keep going during the most troublesome of times. (Tony was a bit of a raconteur himself and now had everyone's attention in the room)

"Are you ready for it?" he asked them. "All I do is focus on my end game goal in life, which is to leave this earth empty one day of everything I could have and should've said or done to some- one by way of encouragement or some form of positivity. My goal is to leave them a little lighter and inspired by my words. And that's it! Now I have that in place, my overall goal or plan, I can now track back to the here and now and set myself daily, weekly, monthly or yearly goals and strive to achieve them. Win or lose, it does not matter as I have my end zone plan carved in stone".

He looked up at all of the guys, hoping for some form of acknowledgement or feedback that something had gone in. To begin with, they were all a little quiet, probably too quiet for Tony's liking. But like a dam that had just been breached by high explosives, signs were beginning to show that finally the penny had dropped and that the guys were starting to get it and appreciate the value of Tony's input. Surprisingly, it was John who spoke first as he felt like a light had just gone on in his head. "You know guys, all these years I've clung on to the notion that football is the be-all and end-all-of-everything. Probably because it's all I've ever known and the only thing I was any good at. But beyond the turnstiles? Oh boy, that's where I feel inadequate and vulnerable. Just thinking about it makes me go weak at the knees," he declared , which kind of shocked the other players and before long they were all talking about and sharing the stuff going on in their world.

The afternoon soon disappeared and was replaced by evening, a rather late evening in fact as the lads could "talk for England" when they got going and Giovanni had to start ushering them out of the door as it was time to lock up and go home. But not before Tony thanked them all for the effort they were putting in at the club, bearing in mind the lack of rewards that had materialised thus far.

"Guys, I'm looking forward to reading about your future goals and dreams for the months and years ahead," and looking at Mac and Mark, he went on to say how the three of them believed in them all and felt sure that this team was destined for great things, but it was up to them as players to start believing it themselves and finally start reaching out for it. The night ended there with lots of back slapping and bear hugging and for the first time everyone sensed a togetherness that had not been there before. The squad genuinely now had each other's back and had forged a bond that could not be easily broken, which was something they so desperately needed especially with some of the teams they were yet to meet in the months ahead.

37

You're live on air, yet again, with HP radio. Interview with the curmudgeon, Mike Phillips and Charles Hayworth.

Charles: HP show host: "Can I have a drum roll please everyone as today we have none other than the great man himself; Mike Phillips"

Mike: "Thanks Charlie. Good to be up and about again!"

Charles: (Under breath) "I see! Charlie? So that's how he wants to play it." Poker face now set and ready for action "Can't imagine Mike, what you have been through in the last year. Tell us; how are things for you right now?" expressed with genuine sincerity.

Mike: "You're right there Chas. It's not been easy. Most blokes would have given up the ghost by now. But not me, I'm a fighter. One of a kind!"

Charles: (Under breath) "Chas now is it? Will probably be C or Big C next!" Back to Mike "Oh, wow, how impressive. Still life in the old dog yet by the sound of it.".

Mike: Slight irritation. Completely non committal. Under breath 'Let's see how he copes with the silent treatment'

Charles: "Oh come on Mike. Not going to go all quiet on me are you? Never had you pegged as the silent type. Tell me; haven't touched a nerve there Mike, have I? On another note; I hear your boy's really shone through at Handley Park these days. You must be so proud."

Mike: Licks his lips slowly and then attempts to clear his throat before responding; "Pity he's not in goal any more as I believe it to be the best position for the lad but that said, he is doing okay considering".

Charles: Probably a little early in the interview, but going in for the kill anyway; "Considering! Considering what Mike? Considering the fact that your lad is now a totally transformed character and no longer wants to pick a fight with the world?"

Mike: "There's nothing wrong with a bit of gumption Charles. I for one am an advocate of spirited men. What's the good book say?" Like iron sharpens iron!".

Charles: "Interesting you say that Mike. So if there was all this sharpening going on, why were Handley Park languishing at the bottom of their league and key players were exiting left, right and centre, as I don't see a lot of gumption in that!"

Mike: Toys from pram now completely strewn across the studio floor "Charles! You seem to have forgotten who you're talking to!"

Charles: "Forgive me Mike, do enlighten me."

Mike: "I give an account to no man. If there is any blame apportion, perhaps you should take that up with Nigel Hawkson. Not me. And for what it's worth, the recent success of the club has only come about because of some of the foundations put in place by me back down the line!"

Charles: "Oh Mike you are priceless! You honestly believe the success of Handley Park Rangers is down to the work you did with the squad over the last two to three seasons?"

Mike: Now deliberately talking over Charles "That is exactly what I am saying! If it hadn't have been for all of the hard work I'd been doing with some of them young lads, well, they just wouldn't be where they are today!"

Charles: Now in total disbelief "Well, it's fair to say that some may consider you delusional. But I myself have found it a real eye opener spending time with you today Mike. Are there any words of wisdom or encouragement you would like to share with the squad over the airways?"

Mike: "Just keep on doing what I've taught you all over the years as it looks to me like all of the hard work we have invested together is finally coming to fruition."

Charles: "Well there you have it folks. Handley Park Rangers, a club at long last going places all thanks to the sterling efforts of; none other than Mike Phillips. Let's hear it for the big man everyone." And with that, Charles quickly turns on a jingle to celebrate the time spent with his special guest.

Needless to say that the local radio station's switchboard was inundated with calls after the interview with Mike. Many angry fans called in live on air to vent their grievances, which of course Charles was more than happy to accommodate. You see, the ultimate plan Charles had in mind was to finally have the man of the moment, Tony Jeffs, on the show.He would be able to not only impart his side of the story but also, and more importantly to at long last shine the light on Charles's career path with the hope of opening the right windows of opportunity with some of the national radio shows. It was a dream he'd had all his life. But for some reason Tony was shunning the limelight and having none of it . 'Surely,' thought Charles,' this latest broadcast would call him out?' After all it couldn't have gone much better once

Mike started running off at the mouth. Alas for now the club remained schtum. But for how much longer? Now that was the question!

38

"We've got him. Well, not quite"

"Are you sure it's him?" asked Tony.

"100%. No doubt whatsoever," replied Big Mac.

"Wow, impressive! How did you manage to find him so quickly?" enquired Tony.

Big Mac rolled in his seat slightly and feigned a cough.

"Oh sorry, mum's the word heh?" chuckled Tony. "No worries. So where is he?"

"Well, he's roughly just over 4 hours away, hiding out in a small fishing village," added Mac.

"Oh, so we can just jump in the car and go and confront him?" suggested Tony.

"No. Just over 4 hours away in a plane to Lanzarote, up on the northern coast near a village called Tenesar," retorted Big Mac.

"So he's not even in the UK? Well that puts paid to that then!" decided Tony.

"So what do you want to do?" boomed Big Mac.

Before Tony had a chance to respond, Mark chipped his pennies worth in. "Not so fast guys. I've been to the Canaries a number of times. In fact, I believe Kieran has substantial business interests out there." There was a moment's pause before the conversation continued.

"What's that got to do with anything?" challenged Big Mac.

Mark was now on his feet and pacing around, desperately trying to figure things out. He stopped in his tracks and turned to both men. Now repeatedly pointing his finger in the air as he spoke "Hold on. Wasn't Kieran recently talking about the team having a small break to recharge the batteries a little?"

" Well yes, but what's that got to do with us finding Nigel?" exclaimed Mac.

You could almost hear the cogs turning in Mark's head as he blurted out "Because." His finger now pointing upwards and bouncing against his nose.

"Because?" smirked Mac restlessly.

"Yes, because Kieran has a business shareholding in a rather large sports complex on the island, if I'm not mistaken ."

"Oh goody gumdrops," replied Mac sarcastically. "What's that got to do with anything?"

With hands now fully outstretched, he looked to Tony for inspiration. Mark's annoying pacing continued before Tony's fist banged his desk. "Maybe," suggested Tony "what Mark is trying to suggest is that we could ask Kieran about the possibility of the squad using the facilities and taking a well deserved break whilst we pop off and confront our friend Nigel."

"Yes, that's it," added a relieved Mark. "D 'you know, the complex is located to the north of the Island as well. It's called Club Les Santos, or something like that, and would be ideal for high altitude training, which would really help the lads build their endurance workout."

"You never know, he may even treat it as a mini break and allow us to invite our partners," added a hopeful Mark.

"Don't get ahead of yourself," remarked Tony "as we've not even asked him yet."

"I know, I know but let's just start thinking those beautiful thoughts," coaxed Mark.

"You and your beautiful thoughts. Honestly!" questioned Mac.

"Look, you focus on how we can interrupt Nigel's day and I will speak with Kieran. D 'you know, he really is a good guy," added Mark "and he just wants to help the club."

"So you keep telling us," responded Mac smugly.

"Chill out you two," retorted Tony trying to break up talk about Kieran as for some reason Mac had his doubts about the man.

"Mac, come on let's focus on how we can create a little surprise for our friend Nigel." "Oh that's simple," confirmed Mac, now pretty keen to strategize a little.

"So, let's assume Mark pulls off the impossible and we manage to whisk ourselves away to a more sunnier climate. Well, first we settle ourselves in at Club Sports or whatever it's called and then we pop out under the cover of darkness for a little recon mission." Tony and Mark instinctively stopped what they were doing and with nodding approval looked at each other with raised eyebrows.

"Soooo! What you're saying Mac is you want, no, I meant, what you need is for me and Tony to come out and help you on a kind of Special Ops mission," asked Mark as both men now started to get a little carried away with themselves. "And what about camouflage? I know of a store in town that sells fatigues. What about war paint for our faces. Have you got any? What about night vision? Can't we get those glasses you strap over your head that makes everything look green? I know, what about a weapon. Will we need one?" Both Mark and Tony were now lost in their own conversation at the prospect of going deep undercover with Big Mac until he could stand it no more and finally cut in.

"You two daydreamers seriously need some help! I was just

talking about killing two birds with one stone and venturing out to confront Nigel and discuss with him how we can grab overall control of the club and hopefully secure some sort of a future for the place." He looked at Mark and Tony who both looked a little crestfallen. Mac sighed deeply before continuing, "Okay, okay you two. Maybe we could mix it up a little while we are out there and plan a little Op, if only to appease you two. Remember it is all about the element of surprise. But no guns!" insisted Mac whilst crossing his body with an outstretched hand.

They all laughed at the thought of their mission, whilst at the same time allowing themselves to be genuinely excited at the prospect of going somewhere hot together to take a break.

"So what's the plan?" quizzed Tony.

"Let me talk to Kieran. I'm seeing him in the morning for a run so I will discuss it then," replied Mark. "Mac, can you mention to the squad about the possibility of us all taking a time out together and see if any time frame will work?" said Tony.

"Will do," responded Mac.

"I was thinking towards the end of the month, which will give us a couple of weeks to sort ourselves out," advised Tony.

"Sounds good to me," noted Mark.

"But one thing!" insisted Tony. "If this idea of Mark's becomes a reality, let's of course make sure we use the time well to put the wind up Nigel, after all, he did leave us in the lurch. But, and more importantly, let's take the time to have a rest and some fun with the lads." They all nodded in agreement knowing that a short time away would do them all the world of good.

"You know," pointed out Mac. "If we get the green light to do this, it couldn't have come at a better time."

Both Tony and Mark looked at Mac perplexed. Mac continued "Do you think we could swing it to invite one of the club's most loyal supporters and one other?" enquired Mac. "Why do you ask?" quizzed Mark.

"Well, I think I've just had a great idea. So see what you can pull out of the hat Mark" challenged Mac.

"Care to elaborate?" mouthed Tony.

"All in good time my friend, all in good time."

And with that the men went about their business before heading off home for the night.

39

A Father's Heart

Without hesitation, Kieran jumped at the chance to get not just the squad but everyone remotely involved with the club out to Lanzarote. He even organised flights, pickups to and from the airport and arranged for luxury accommodation at the resort, but on one proviso! That he and his wife could join in on the fun. It truly was a great opportunity for everyone, which was probably why nobody needed to be asked twice about whether they fancied or could manage to book some time off for, a proposed jolly up in the sun. In fact, not one person encountered any obstacles regarding a getaway from work and before they knew it, just over 40 Handley Park Rangers were jetting off for a luxury midweek break. Even John Vossa managed to encourage his somewhat hectic wife to take time away from their young children and join him for a well deserved rest together.

Soon after arriving at the airport, they were met by a small welcoming party who'd organised coaches to transfer them to their resort. The luxury of a well equipped coach did not go unnoticed, as the squad had yet to experience the pleasure of travelling to a match in an air conditioned vehicle (all except

John of course). Either way, such a simple gesture was very much appreciated by all. Once at the resort, the party soon went off to find their rooms, as later that morning Mark had organised a short trek for the squad along a rather picturesque coastline to help them acclimatize.

In the meantime, the group took full advantage of the water sports and were soon jet skiing or kayaking across the bay. Much later in the evening, everyone met for a traditional cena in one of the many restaurants situated within the complex grounds. The food, of course, was first class and appreciated by all, accept the club's extra guest Giovanni, who managed to find fault with the freshly sourced vegetables. This was much to the annoyance of his beautiful young daughter, Allegra.

After their meal, Clay along with John and Mac, managed to convince a rather shy Sam to stop hiding out in his room for the night and join them for a leisurely stroll along the sea front. It really was a glorious evening as the last of the sun's rays shimmered across the calmest of seas and the feel of the soft sand on their bare feet felt so intoxicating. The four of them sauntered in silence, allowing the cool sea water to gently wash their sand covered feet. Their peace, however, was short lived as they were soon joined by the rather over excited Darren and Frank who took it upon themselves to lay down the gauntlet and "take a shot at the title" by attempting to topple Clay "The Man Mountain" Jackson; all in the hope of submerging him in the sea for a good old fashioned soaking. But of course, they were the ones who ended up drinking a cocktail of seawater and sand as Clay politely suggested they yield by gently holding the back of their heads below the surface of the water. With all of this going on, Mac and John took the time to sit amongst some sand dunes with Sam and watch the last of the sun's presence disappear behind the horizon.

"How you getting on Sam? You enjoying yourself?" asked John.

"Oh most definitely," replied Sam. "This place is something else."

"It certainly is," sighed Mac. "Have you had a chance to catch up with anyone?"

"Oh yeah," responded Sam. "I've had a good chat with Tony and Helen and Kieran and his wife."

"Ah that's nice," assured John. "Anyone else? What about Giovanni? Have you had a chance to catch up with him?"

Now shaking his head and looking a bit sheepish, Sam went on to explain how he'd not had the chance yet plus, of course, Mark had quite an itinerary planned and was keeping them all busy with circuit training.

"Yeah, I understand," advised John. "It's not easy always making time on a paradise island."

"Well, I wouldn't quite put it like that, "began Sam.

"So John, what about you? Have you managed to catch up at all with Giovanni? Oh, and what about his rather beautiful daughter? Now what was her name? Ah, Allegra I do believe. Have you spoken with her? You know she is rather lovely. And such fun to be around!" remarked Mac to John.

"Funny you should say that Mac as I had a wonderful chat with Allegra and her dad earlier," concurred John.

Sam could stand it no more and forced himself forward vertically as his feet struggled for stability in the sand. In the process, he sprayed both John and Mac head to toe with sand.

"Look, I know what you two are trying to do and it won't wash with me," retorted Sam.

"Oh yeah and what's that?" queried Mac.

Sam, now pointing and wagging his finger at the two men whilst slowly backing away, replied "Listen, I'll talk to her, but in my own time, when I'm good and ready, all right!" "Okay, okay, keep your hair on," declared John. "But remember, we're only here 'til Friday and at the rate you're going you'll need til Christmas to pluck up the courage."

"That's not fair," shouted Sam sulkily. "I'm not afraid you know, I just want to get the moment right, that's all."

"Well, it looks to me son, that your moment has just arrived," said Mac discreetly pointing over Sam's shoulder. And as he turned, he spotted Allegra walking along the beach with her dad. Sam felt slightly faint. His first thought was to "man right up" and let the world know that "Sam the man was not the type of guy who ran" but after a quick reality check, he opted for his safer plan B strategy of pegging it for dear life. However, his two supposed companions, had already preempted young Sam and blocked his exit route. With no other options to take, Sam was now beginning to panic inside and was desperate for some form of help. He looked at both Mac and Sam fully expecting them to turn the vice by continuing to ridicule him, yet again. In fairness though, he knew their efforts were well intentioned but the "party bus of banter" just wasn't doing it for him. Surprisingly, when he finally met their gaze he realised that all they were trying to do was help him take a risk by stepping out of his comfort zone, whilst egging him on a little. He looked again in Allegra's direction and then back to Mac and John desperately hoping one of them would bail him out but of course they weren't going to.

"Oh, hi Giovanni, Allegra. I did not expect to see you guys out this evening!" said John with a rather velvety tone.

"Yes, that's right, me neither. Isn't it a lovely evening?" stated Big Mac rather scriptedly.

"You a know," responded Giovanni; "this is a justa what the doctor ordered, I feel so, what is the word? Relaxed." Pausing for a minute, Giovanni, looking somewhat confused, looked around before continuing;,"I thought I saw three of you standing there a minute ago."

Now side by side, John and Big Mac looked at each other before taking a step apart to reveal a rather cowering looking Sam behind them.

"Oh a good evening Sam," says Giovanni "is a there any reason why a you are kneeling behind your a two friends in the sand? It a looks to me a as if you were hiding!"

Sam, now casually getting to his feet, attempted to save face by announcing that of course he wasn't hiding as he'd been rather busy searching in the sand for a lost contact lense.

"Oh, I wasn't aware you wore contact lenses. Must have been fairly recent then!" mused John who quickly regretted his comments when Mac casually kneed him in the shins. "You a need some help there son?" pronounced Giovanni whilst gently blocking Allegra's path to assist him.

However, she soon got her way by dancing round her father's rather futile efforts and was soon crouching on the ground to help. After a time, Sam quickly whispered in her ear that he did not really wear contact lenses to which Allegra replied that she already knew that and before long they were soon walking along the water's edge engrossed in conversation. Giovanni, now out of earshot, turned to Mac and John and asked

"Are you sure, Mac, this lad is a good one?"

"Without a doubt Giovanni, I vouch for him 100%. I knew his dad well as we were in the forces together," replied Mac.

"Yeah, I can vouch for him too," added John.

Giovanni, now looking seriously at both men replied "You, I trust implicitly as a good judge of character," he motioned a finger pointing at Mac. "But your assessment," now pointing at John "is not a worth diddly squat based on a that fool Stan that runs your luxury used car centre."

An uncomfortable silence ensued, which included John with his mouth wide open aghast. But before John could even consider reacting, Mac and Giovanni burst out laughing and were soon on their knees, in the sand, trying to control themselves.

"I'm a so sorry John," declared Giovanni whilst holding his aching sides at the same time. "He," now pointing to Mac "put a me up to it." which was all he could manage to say before a fit of laughter consumed him once more.

Finally, the penny dropped and John realised he'd been had by the two old timers and before long he was rounding on Big Mac, preparing to launch a counteroffensive. Once again though, he was easily hood winked by Mac as he pointed in the distance suggesting that maybe he could see Becky over yonder, and with that, Mac, as quick as lightning, was on his toes running back in the direction of the hotel. It wasn't long though before John was quickly on his tail, as he was keen to avenge with a clean rugby tackle straight into the surf. With those two now out of the picture, Giovanni gestured to Allegra that maybe he could have a minute with Sam. Now looking squarely into Sam's eyes he declared "I a like you Sam. You a may be a bit rough round the edges but I believe you a have a good heart. Allegra likes you too," which made Sam's cheeks flush a little at the thought. "But let's not, how'd you put it? Jump the gun!" he continued. "So we take a things nice and slowly! Okay?"

"Okay," agreed Sam.

"No interrupt, I've not finished," continued Giovanni. Sam was now looking quite subservient towards Allegra's dad. " So, you take good care of my daughter yeh? You get her home on time and then maybe my sons not kill you!" Giovanni laughed.

 Sam tried not to look too concerned.

"I only kidding Sam; they wouldn't kill you! No! I would!" Giovanni laughed again whilst Sam winced at the prospect.

"I only make joke again," pronounced Giovanni. "Good talk though, yes, good talk!" And with that, the old man sighed deeply to himself, shook his head and slowly turned to leave his daughter with Sam. He knew instinctively that Big Mac and John were right about the lad and that the pretence of a chance encounter, on the beach, instigated by all three men was a good choice. But with all that said, it still pained him to trust another with one so precious.

As a saddened Giovanni neared the hotel, he was joined by a rather exhausted and soaked through Mac and John. Mac was about to state that he'd never have had Giovanni pegged as a stool pigeon, but instinctively could tell by the look of his old friend, that he was weighed down by his decision to allow his daughter to spend time with Sam. With a discreet gesture to John, both men, now either side of Giovanni, fell in step with him, walking in silence. As they reached the steps of the sports complex, Giovanni finally spoke "It a would be much easier for me if I a did not like this lad! Alas I am not able to! He has been raised well. I know, as you say, that he has a chequered past, but who hasn't? This is very tough for me. I even threaten the lad and all he does is pay me respect. I blame you two! Yes, that is right! And for that you owe me two large drinks. Yes, a nightcap I think, at the bar."

" I can live with that," accepted John "after all it was Big Mac's idea. Come on Mac, get your wallet out."

And before Mac had a chance to respond, a drink's menu was thrust in his hand and all three men were guided through a vignette of foliage and out onto the veranda.

40

The Three Amigos.

"I thought we'd been through this and agreed that there would be no wearing of camouflage fatigues!" barked a rather grouchy Mac as he climbed into their super mini rental, wearing a somewhat tacky bright yellow T-shirt, blue shorts and flip flops.

"Never had you pegged as the touristy type!" ridiculed Mark.

Mac shot Mark an "if looks could kill" stare before countering "Never had you down as a groupie for The Village People."

"Woah, hold the phone you guys! Remember why we are here, ease up!" cautioned Tony.

It was a little after five in the morning and the men had left the confines of their comfy beds and were now heading due north in the hope of a staged "shock and awe" tactic for one Nigel Hawkson. It truly was a beautiful morning and far too early for the cicadas to make an appearance with their high-pitched humming. The panoramic view of the volcanic landscape was simply stunning but the chaps weren't out to make memories. No, they were on a mission. The journey took them no more than 40 minutes at best, with no detours which was purely down to Mac's natural navigating ability. Now, no more than a 10 minute drive from Nigel's hide out, Mac had them pull over in a lay-by. He wanted to go over the plan one more time, which, as far as Mark was concerned was ludicrous as his view was simple; let's get him out of bed and confront the man who'd caused so much upset at the club.

"You know," remarked a rather disgruntled Mac "he must have siphoned off tens of thousands of pounds in the last 6 to 8 months."

"No, way more," cut in Tony. "It's tough guys, I know, but I just need some answers and, if we can, a chance to draw a line in the sand and move on."

"And if you don't like what you hear?" remarked Mark.

"Well, we'll just have to invoke Plan B!" replied Tony.

"Which is?" insisted Mac.

"To be honest, I don't know yet. But one thing is for sure; we're fast learners!" declared Tony.

"That's for sure!" chipped in Mac.

"Hear, hear!" added Mark.

"Right then. Let's get going!" roared Mac, and before they knew it, like a rat up a drainpipe he was out of the car and climbing a rather secluded dirt track that spiralled the top of a hillside. The trek took about 20 minutes and led them to an electric-gated, rather charming looking villa with spectacular views across the North Atlantic ocean.

"Figures!" snorted Mac venomously. "Looks like he's been slumming it again!"

"Well, not for much longer as I reckon his numbers up!" remarked Tony as he stepped forward and rattled the small access gate to the side of the main entrance.

"Steady!" whispered Mac. "Let's not spoil the element of surprise!"

The men made their way along a walled garden that led them

past an impressive looking Infinity style outdoor pool.

"Now, that looks inviting right now," declared a somewhat hot and bothered Mark.

"Arh, bit hot are we?" sniggered Mac.

Not one to shy away from banter, Mark responded "Bring it on old timer as I'm just getting warmed up."

Tony, not in the mood snapped, "Listen you two, just button it for a minute and put your handbags away as I think there may be a way in over there."

Now pointing, he moved towards an old style, brick built grotto: a neo-classical pediment discreetly hidden away by some moss covered trees. Now nicely out of view, the three men weight tested a precarious looking old wall attached to the side of the grotto. Satisfied with its load bearing capacity, Mac took a step back in preparation for a run up. And with a quick one, two he clambered on top. Shortly after, he was offering a hand to help the others up. Mac, now most definitely in the zone, ventured ahead by skipping his way atop a flanked moss covered wall. After dismounting, he crouched low before peeking through lush ferns for a closer look. They were now no more than 8-10 metres away from the pool side. He turned to the guys and without realising it, instinctively commenced visual signalling with his hands. Although completely baffled, the two men, now enjoying the military style communique, both dropped to their knees and assumed a kind of combat position. Perplexed at what they were doing, Mac mouthed to them both that they should get themselves over to him on the double.

"What on earth were you two doing hitting the deck like that?" commented a somewhat exasperated Mac.

"Well, we weren't sure what you were trying to say so just assumed that maybe we'd been compromised or something."

Shaking his head he pointed "Looks like we are in business as

one of those double doors under the canopy is open over there."
Soon after, the three Amigos, like liberators of an occupied
nation, made their way through the open door and into what was
obviously an air-conditioned lounge area. Now moving about the
place with trepidation, the men searched the vast living space
expecting to stumble upon Nigel, but there was no sign of him.
They soon found themselves at the bottom of a marble, spiral
staircase when what sounded like a conveyor belt burst into life.
The noise, from what they could tell, originated on the upstairs
landing where it seemed to quickly gather momentum. After a
short recce Mac hid behind a marble pillar whilst Tony and Mark
ducked behind an elegant Chesterfield sofa. The not so distant,
noise continued for what felt like an age before finally coming to
a complete stop just above the Bullnose step. And after a bit of
groaning and shuffling, the sound of rubber could be heard as it
squelched across the marble floor. Instinctively, Mac recognised
the sound as that of a wheelchair in motion and without hesitating, decided to give away his position by standing to his feet to
find out who the occupant of the chair was. After what seemed
like an absolute age, he casually spoke, "Hello Nigel."
Of course, they'd achieved what they had set out to do, which
was to namely catch Nigel off guard. But what they hadn't
bargained for, was to find themselves equally as surprised. You
see, Nigel was in very poor health. In fact, his body was so badly
ravaged with sickness and infection, he'd decided to hide
somewhere peaceful to see out, what he thought were his
remaining days. A heavy silence descended upon the room as no
one knew quite what to say. Tony and Mark slowly stood up
from their hiding places and joined Mac. The three men stared at
Nigel for what seemed like an eternity before the silence was
interrupted by what appeared to be a nurse or carer, who came
in speaking loudly in Spanish as she attempted to usher the men

from her patient's presence. However, Nigel soon silenced her with a half hearted attempt to quell her concerns. His voice was restrained as he gestured to the woman, Rosa, that he knew the men and that all was well.

Nigel did attempt to speak first but it was Tony who led the way by tactfully enquiring as to his well being. Nigel nonchalantly replied that he was near the end of his road. "How near?" interjected a less tactful Big Mac.

Tony gave Mac his best Paddington Bear stare of disapproval but Nigel just raised his hand stating that it was "Okay Tony. In fact," he continued "it was more than overdue. These last 6-8 months or so I've treated you men so badly and with such disrespect. I don't know what to say."

"Well, you can start by telling us where the hundreds of thousands of pounds have gone from the Club's bank account?" declared a rather disgruntled Mac.

Nigel looked to the polished floor and began fidgeting with his hands "Experimental life prolonging drugs I'm afraid gentlemen."

"And how did that fair for you?" remarked Mac.

"It didn't," was all Nigel said.

There was a moment's pause before someone spoke "D'you know Nigel? It didn't have to be this way. You could have let us in and given us the chance to get involved. In fact, instead of dissin us you could have joined forces with us," declared a frustrated Tony. Mark finally entered the fray by asking where Todd was in all of this. Nigel's somewhat softer looking eyes narrowed for a split second as he considered his boy but he soon cast the thought aside by replying "What does he have to do with any of this?"

"Because I think he has a right to know that his father is gravely ill" sighed Mark. "Look," mumbled a rather emotional Nigel "let's just call it what it is! I'm done, I've lost everything including my wife and my boy and I've abused my power as owner of the club by siphoning off what I could lay my hands on."

"That's probably a fair assessment," chipped in Mac.

"But it could have been worse!"

All eyes were now on Mark before Mac countered "Oh yeah! And how so?"

"Well, if Mike Phillips was still at the helm you would have had nothing, including no club!"

It did take a minute or two for those pearls of wisdom to sink in but eventually all four men found themselves smirking at the thought. It was a little unclear as to why they found it amusing, but it did seem to have the desired effect and at long last had them all talking openly about how they really felt. Which did include Nigel candidly explaining why he chose Tony in the first place. "I'm sorry Tony, but you were the only option available, plus I thought your lack of ability as a coach would help plunge the club into free-fall."

"What do you mean hopefully?" replied Mac. "It already was in freefall," which had the men laughing again.

Soon it was time for the men to leave as it was pretty obvious that Nigel's strength was waning but before leaving, Tony left Nigel with this thought "I can't say what is going to happen here Nigel. You've upset and let down a lot of people at the club. But, and more importantly, I do think you should consider making contact with your son. In the meantime, if you will allow me the time to speak with all of those concerned at the club well then maybe, I think you should consider coming home and facing the music as I think there is still a little bit of fight left in the old dog yet. But that decision is, of course, up to you! As for me, I plan to go back to my apartment and serenade my wife before returning to the UK and rolling the dice, once again in the hope that we will make it through to the next round of the cup and beyond."

And with that the men parted company leaving Nigel to his own thoughts. Of course he'd felt embarrassed getting all his dirty laundry out like that and telling them what had been going on in his world, but truth be told, it was the most alive and invigorated he'd felt in a long time. That Tony definitely had a way about him and made it seem all so simple. But go home, call my boy and face the music? This guy's thoughts were off the charts. 'But what if he was right?' pondered Nigel. Either way he had to do something as he could no longer hide away here and if he was being honest with himself, he didn't want to as he missed home.

41

A Band of Brothers! (5th Round Proper)

It was late February and the lads were on their way to south London to meet an elite Premiership side, who'd recently had a change of personnel due to a fairly heavy slide in form. Their "waiting in the wings" successor had a point to prove as his name had just been dragged through the mire due to a rather unfortunate incident involving some undercover reporters leading him down a somewhat, dark, murky path that would eventually end his short tenure as head coach of a prestigious team. That said, this chap had been round the block and knew a thing or three about how to extract the best from his players, even if they were lacking in form and self belief. This would by far be the toughest challenge yet for Handley Park who, of course, had exceeded all expectations thus far by reaching this stage in the competition. In fact, as much as it was a David and Goliath saga for many, so to was it an embarrassment for those at the highest level. It was deemed that the sooner these amateurs were eliminated from the cup, the better it would be, for not just the Pros but for the beautiful game itself.

It was an evening kick off so the lads had grouped together and gone up in convoy with 5 cars, well 4 cars plus Sam's van to be precise, as Graham's rather unreliable estate car (or sport tourer as he liked to call it) had, whilst on the way back from work, finally died. In the weeks building up to the game, the lads had been pushed hard by the running man, having them meet at least twice a week to train as well as three early mornings to jog up into the hills just outside of town. The only exception to the rule for this intensive training module had been John Vossa and that was purely because his legs, along with the rest of his body, were no longer up to the rigours of high tempo training. Instead, he maintained a fairly low key cardiovascular workout within the confines of his own personal fitness gym at home. But what he lacked in physical endurance was easily surpassed by an alert footballing mind that could still read a game extremely well. This, coupled with his pinpoint passing and playmaking ability, still made him an incredible force for any team, let alone Handley Park. In fact, for some time now, representation from South East Asia had been making noises about offering a ludicrous amount to entice him out of his supposed retirement. For now though, that decision was well and truly on the back burner as tonight the lads had a job to do.

So, after the preliminary pre-show warm ups and kick about in front of an expectant home crowd who, it had to be said, were likely to accept no more than a three nil routing of these part timers, the lads headed back to their changing room, where they would strip and wait to be inspired by yet another one of Tony's "British-bulldog spirit" chats. However, this time they were encouraged to sit in silence and asked to close their eyes and zone out for at least a minute or two before being told to create a low pitched humming noise, deep in the back of their throats whilst simultaneously beating their chest, in a rhythmic aggressive style. Of course, it was all off the charts stuff which was pretty much the norm for Tony. But the players had somehow, over time, become almost accustomed to his idiosyncrasies. In fact, they kind of embraced his motivational tactics as it had the effect of dispersing any signs of inhibitions, whilst at the same time making them feel at home with each other. Before long, the out of tune humming was replaced by the sound of the 8 minute buzzer informing them it was time to go. Instinctively, the squad rose to their feet prepared and ready for business. But for some reason tonight, the mood had intensified. Not because of the chest beating and humming (although it did seem to create a warm fuzzy feeling inside). No, it was something different. It was as if the team had consciously surpassed a state of tolerance for one another, instead replacing it with a sense of unity but at a far more profound level of understanding and acceptance of one another. This in turn forced a state of euphoria, as it no longer mattered who they had to face as they would all face them together. No longer were these lads a bunch of part time wanna-bes. No, they were a force to be reckoned with and all three coaches were lapping it up knowing that it was a culmination of good old fashioned sweat and toil that had gotten them all here. Tonight was going to be a good night.

Sadly though, the first period of the game did not live up to expectations. In fact, the first half produced very little in the way of excitement as both styles of play proved reticent as any attempts at playmaking were soon cancelled out by, arguably two very in form midfields. The battle for possession was yet to be won as the middle of the pitch was crowded-out, allowing very little in the way of time or space to move the ball around. During Handley Park's half time team talk, the coaches spoke of not wanting to leave this place empty handed nor, for that matter, were they prepared to accept a token replay at home. So the question raised was "What options do we have lads?" Silence descended upon the room. Mac challenged again;"Come on you lot: Normally you love the sound of your own voice. What are our options?"

Finally Graham, the club's striker spoke "Err, to win".

Then out came Mark with his Widow Twankey voice "I can't hear you!" followed by a few grumblings. Widow Twankey chipped in again "I can't hear you" and at long last the penny dropped and more voices responded "To win!!"

"Again!!" shouted Mac. "But this time own it!"

"To win!" shouted the lads.

"That's more like it!!" confirmed Mac. "Now I want to change things up a little. Our defence has held firm but I'm sure if the opposition manages to get the ball out from midfield to their wingers, then we'll start to feel the pressure so let's "chuck em' a curve ball" as I suspect they will be making some changes in the centre of that crowded park. I want to bring both wings back into the game and have them running the lines but instead of running for the by-lines, I want them cutting inside as we enter their half of the field and feeding our central men. Let's now focus our run of play by deliberately channelling all traffic through John. Graham, I know you've done a sterling job but I want you now to offer a support role to John and help him to force a path through that rather crowded midfield and perhaps create the breakthrough we need to hit them where it hurts." Mac now turned and looked directly at John. "From here on in John, this is your show. I need you to leave everything you have on the field of play by using the players you have moulded around you and let's depart this place with the result we deserve and the quarter finals well and truly in our sights."

And as the players made their way out to the tunnel, Tony pulled John to one side "This is it John."

"I know," added John.

Tony replied "No, you don't. You see John, this game is the catalyst that will catapult this team to the next level and you, our ageing warrior, are that catalyst." John, somewhat confused, tried to reply "What do you mean catalyst?"

Tony, now looking rather profoundly into John's eyes said "This, my friend, is where you will lay down your ghost and see a life for you beyond football," and before John could utter a reply he was gone.

From the moment the second half whistle blew Handley Park, who'd taken heed to Big Mac's words, changed the way they were set up and started channelling the ball through John via their wing backs. Initially, it looked as if John had not read the memo as he just did not seem up for the challenge, but as the game reached the one hour mark the football genius that once was jumped into life. It was as if the dormant force within John seemed to spark into gear as he began to hit his top range and at long last the game finally burst into life. It was an absolute joy to watch, as John completely overwhelmed the midfield, opening up their defence at will with perfectly timed and weighted through balls. And before long, Graham and Sam, who up until now had been mere spectators, broke the last line of defence and with a simple one-two rounded the keeper and Handley Park, at long last, had their noses in front.

The next ten minutes of play were crucial for the team to not only not concede but to keep their momentum and shape without losing their nerve. Now, with just over five minutes of play left, Handley Park won a direct free kick right on the edge of the box. It was skilfully taken by Frank as he passed the ball directly under their defensive wall and right into the path of John, who immediately turned, shimmied one defender before "nutmegging" another and with only the yellow jerseyed number 1 to beat, instinctively lowered his head and raised an arm to guide the ball beyond. But just as his favourite left foot descended, he felt an acute pain in his right knee. In fact, John was not able to finish his shot as unbeknown to him, his right knee cap had dislodged, vacating its socket by at least 45 degrees leaving him spread eagled on the floor and in a great deal of pain. Play was quickly stopped and panic stricken players from both sides soon merged and rallied round John, trying not to look squeamish at the sight of his injury whilst offering some form of comfort. John soon had a team of medics around him trying to quickly ascertain the extent of his injury. It was quickly decided that he should be stretchered off and sent directly to hospital to carry out a reduction or in other words to manipulate his kneecap back into place and establish if there were any other underlying injuries. But John, although in severe pain, was having none of it. Instead he challenged the advice of the medic (who'd already explained to him that he was not qualified to put the kneecap back into position) and called for team mates Graham, the clubs appointed first aider, and Clay to come over. Eventually, the medics acquiesced to John's demands and granted him a brief moment with his team mates. When finally alone, he came straight to the point. "I need your help guys. I need you to manipulate my knee back into place; here and now." He definitely had their full attention now as he continued. "Will you help me?"

Both Clay and Graham, slightly aghast, looked at each other with concern before Graham responded "Have you completely lost your mind? Let's get this right. You are asking us, no I stand corrected, me, to manipulate your knee back into place, in front

of fifty thousand prying eyes so you can carry on playing."
Graham added for good measure "Have I got that right?"
Clay added "You've forgotten those watching by TV."
John quickly gave Clay a 'looks could kill' glance. John was in no
mood for small talk. "Okay Graham. Are you in or are you out?"
he shouted over his pain. "Can you fix the knee and help get me
back on my feet so I can finish this game?"
Graham looked like a rabbit in the headlights of a car. He rubbed
his stubbly chin whilst looking to Clay for moral support. Clay in
return met with Graham's eyes expressing a knowing look that
informed him that whatever choice he made, Clay would back
him. Finally Graham spoke "You know John, if this goes wrong, I
could be in a whole lot of trouble."
"I know," confirmed John "I wouldn't normally ask, but this is
something I really need to do." Clay now chipped in "Why do
you need to risk it all now, for this game?"
Without hesitation John responded "Listen Clay. The simple
answer is, without hesitation, I'd risk everything for you guys.
You know in all my years, I've never met such a bunch of misfits
but for some unknown reason I seem to fit and I truly love you
all like brothers. In fact, my short time with you lot has meant
more to me than the last 15 years as a professional player. It just
does not make sense." John was quite emotional now so Graham
swiftly put two fingers directly to John's lips. His brain was now
churning as he worked through his options before he finally
responded "Clay, I need your large frame along with some of the
other guys to help ward off any prying-eyes." "You got it," said
Clay and beckoned some of the lads.
Graham looked down at John "You know, I won't be able to
access their gas and air to help with your pain relief."
"I know," said John.
Graham leaned in towards John and spoke again "Do you know

how painful this is likely to be if I manipulate your leg? I can sugar coat my answer if you like." John just gestured before Graham continued "We're talking labour pain territory and that's assuming there is no break beneath."

John replied "I think I'd prefer the sugar coated response."

Graham replied "That was the sugar coated version" and all three men forced a kind of nervous laughter before Graham asked Clay to arrange for the players to create a shield and make some noise by talking among themselves rather loudly.

"It's likely you'll hear the equivalent screams of a woman's labour pain shortly," gestured Graham. And with that, he knelt down by John's leg and with Clay the other side, he explained how he would countdown from three and then begin the procedure. They gave John a quick swig of water before commencing the countdown. So with Clay holding John firmly one side and John trying desperately to mentally prepare, they began. Graham spoke "Here we go three..." but John cut in "Do you mean on three or after three?"

"What does it matter?" cried Graham somewhat flustered.

Clay gave Graham a look of disapproval before he continued "Okay, okay, we'll go on three!"

A relieved John said "Good, good, let's go, I'm ready."

"Right," panted Graham, "here we go three..." and before they had a chance to get to two Graham, rather proficiently grabbed the out of place kneecap and guided it back into place. The deafening high pitched scream that emerged from John's mouth soon had the medics attention. Before long, they were surrounded by the medical team wanting to know what exactly was going on, but by then both Clay and Graham had forced John to his feet and were supporting him from either side. The chief medic demanded to know what was going on as this man, pointing to John, was under his care but John replied by telling the medic that he was fine and pushed Clay and Graham away from his side to prove that he could stand on his own.

"It was just a nasty fall doc, that winded me, that's all. I plan to thank my friend (he bellowed rather menacingly as he looked toward Graham) later."

The medic continued "Well, okay then. Are you sure you are alright?" he asked rather dubiously looking at them all.

"Yes absolutely, never better," snapped John trying to convince himself more than those around him and then he proceeded to carry out some stretches before making his way back toward the centre circle. And as John hobbled along there was a stirring in the crowd as people stood to their feet and began spontaneously applauding him. Before long, the entire stadium were shouting and cheering his name and as a reward John responded by jumping and dancing in rhythm to their chants which made the crowd even louder. Play eventually reconvened, with what was best described as a party atmosphere; wave after Mexican wave undulated around the stadium coupled with a deafening noise powerful enough to take the roof off. Thankfully Handley Park held on to their lead and the game ended with all 22 players converged in the centre circle, pretty much just enjoying the moment whilst celebrating both Handley Park's victory along with John's bravado. It was a memorable evening.

Back in the changing room and after John had finished squeezing Graham in a headlock, Tony, Mac and Mark stood before the lads. Once the chants and jubilation had subsided he finally spoke "Do any of you know what's etched on the wall at the entrance of Handley Park?"

Darren cleared his throat and spoke "Ain't it some kind of Latin word De gio something or other?"

The lads laughed at Darren's exaggerated pronunciation.

"Nice try Darren, the words are actually Deo Iuvante. Does

anyone know what that means?" Silence descended so Tony continued "It means 'with God's help' and I reckon that's exactly what has been going on here lads, these past few months. Against the backdrop of every kind of adversity, we have been helped to keep going and stay together. With God's help, 3 raving lunatics tonight broke every rule in the medical journal and managed to keep us all together. Let's not take for granted the hand that is upon us and make sure we maximise every moment. So, who's ready for the next opportunity?" And with that the room erupted with all of the men bundling on top of poor old Graham.

42

The Quarter Final - Sisu - True Grit

The initial quarter final tie was held at a Championship stadium in Surrey, where Handley Park Rangers squandered countless goal-scoring opportunities resulting in the game ending goalless. However, the team thankfully managed to score a great moral victory in terms of their defensive play. You see, historically Handley Park Rangers had suffered with what you would call a dearth of defenders, but not now. After all, Big Mac had spent a lot of time with his back three in training and introducing them to yet another one of his historical characters. This time, it was the turn of a biblical character called Nehemiah and his quest to rebuild a stone wall of defence around what was once his beloved fortified hometown, that was now lying in ruins. But of course in the lad's case, it was no more than a penalty area. He'd tasked each of them with being responsible and accountable for the area of play directly in front of them, including the involvement of any key players to support them during their quest to protect their territory. The defence were also tasked with coping with stressful, pressurised and often difficult situations but without being penalised or accruing any yellow or red cards. And you know what? It really paid off for them as their defensive play throughout was exceptional and by the end of the game their opposition's attempts at goal proved futile.

The replay however, would be a different kettle of fish altogether. During the first tie, Handley Park had shown its trump card of 'all out defensive play' and mounting a quick counter attack when the opportunity presented itself, so this time they needed to mix things up a little and that was why Big Mac tasked the starting eleven with a stealthy shock and awe tactic. This involved moving forward as a unit with such a high tempo of play that of course could not be sustained, but with the express hope of snatching an early lead, ideally, within the first 45 minutes of play. It was a huge risk, but if successful, the lads would then be tasked with battening down the hatches in the form of solid defensive manoeuvres, breaking up opposition play and looking to counter. In theory, the plan seemed a viable idea but putting the plan into practise, like anything, would always be a challenge.

The replay was held at Handley Park and was watched by the club's largest crowd to date. Some 2000 spectators crammed into the still dilapidated Hawker Tempest stand, as well as the "open to the elements"Hurricane Alley and Vickers End terraces. There were countless TV trucks strewn across the main car park behind the privacy hedges and a makeshift studio had been erected high above the main bar to the right of the single turn style. The return match had been dubbed by the pundits as the ultimate "Grudge rematch" between the minos; "Handley Park Rangers" and the mighty sporting elite of this well known, historic, tier 2 club. Against all odds, the shock and awe tactics paid dividends as within the first 10 minutes of play, Handley Park drew blood with a sensational solo effort by Sam from deep within his own half. He'd run right through the centre of the midfield and as he breached the edge of the opposition's box, he played a nice one-two with Graham before completing an impressive shimmy which wrong footed one of their most experienced centre backs. This allowed Sam the time to look up and place the ball nicely in the top corner, beyond the reach of the outstretched glove of their number 1 keeper. Sure enough, the speed of play and subsequent goal conceded stunned their opponents and left them shell shocked for the rest of the first half.

After the break, the following 45 minutes proved much the same as the opposition struggled to steady the ship and find their regular flow of play, so as the clock reached 75 minutes of the final 90, their well respected, Italian coach made the brave decision of bringing on all 3 substitutions at the same time. It was a very spirited move; sacrificing a key central defensive player, along with 2 midfielders, in favour of some much needed fresh legs in attack supported by two wingers that would now surely open up Handley's defence.

The changes made had an immediate impact and Handley Park Rangers soon found themselves on the back foot for the first time in the game. Wave after wave of attacks were launched at their weary and rather battered defence. It held firm, but the signs of fatigue were starting to show as Clay now found himself the busiest player on the park. Shots on target were now well into double figures but Clay, as usual, proved himself worthy of the challenge. Handley's rookie of a left back, Ryan, had collapsed to the floor writhing in agony from muscle cramp, which proved a blessing as it gave the team a breather before play recommenced. As the ball was out of play, an opposing player, as an act of sportsmanship, passed the ball back to Clay which allowed him to utilise the full extent of the penalty area before launching one of his clinical quarterback throws right to the feet of what was now their lone attacker. Graham skillfully brought the ball under control with the intention of heading to the corner flag and wasting as much time as possible in order to run the clock down. This in turn allowed Handley Park the chance to re-group and at long last venture out of their own half and towards the opposition goal. However, this proved a costly mistake. Graham was easily shoved off the ball by a rather burly defender who quickly launched the ball beyond virtually all of the Handley Park players directly into the path of the most expensive player on the park. He'd timed his run to perfection by beating the offside trap with ease and was now frantically heading towards Handley Park's penalty area. Thankfully, Darren managed to steer the striker away to the left of goal, which created precious time for his teammates to catch up with this rather effective counter-attack. However, Darren soon found himself the wrong side of goal as the striker changed direction and turned on the inside of him, allowing just enough time for a beautifully weighted diagonal cross that sliced through the returning defence and beyond the outstretched left boot of Handley's last man and into the path of one of the Championships most prolific goal scorers. Not one to look a gift horse in the mouth, the striker hit the ball, instinctively and with such venom on the volley. The shot was a moment of pure class as the ball was soon heading away from Clay and into the net. But Clay, being Clay, wasn't quite ready to concede a goal at such a late stage in the game and by using his rather understated skills of body movement he was able to force both arms down onto the goal line which gave him enough force to unleash his legs with a backward flick in such an unorthodox manner that somehow managed to intercept the goal-bound ball and clear it off the line and nicely to the feet of a Handley Park player.

Big Mac had been pacing up and down the technical area when Clay pulled off his last save. He was convinced an equaliser had been scored and had instinctively coiled his body away from the pitch with such disappointment, especially after the hard fought battle the players had endured. But when he saw the response of both Tony and Mark and the rest of the players on the bench, he quickly spun on his heels to view what was going on. The fans were chanting in pure delight at the marvel of such an ostentatious save and most of Handley Park subs had run on the pitch to congratulate Clay but, of course, he just took it all in his stride, describing it as no more than a fortunate run of play. But, as usual, the team knew better and jumped on Clay in jubilation. 'One day,' Mac thought to himself, 'they'll be able to topple the towering Clay if they all managed to jump on him.' He looked down to check the time on his watch and gave a sideways glance to Tony and Mark, acknowledging to them both the full 90 minutes were about up. All three of them waited with baited breath just in case a rather long, drawn out Fergie-time was announced but as no real incidents had occurred during the second half, no more than a minute of extra play was announced and so Handley Park just adopted the procedure of complete ball possession with the simple aim of running down the clock. And within no time at all, the final whistle blew and with that, the entire team congregated around their dugout to celebrate such an amazing achievement.

Later on in the changing room, it took a little time for the men to quieten down but eventually after some persuasive threats from Big Mac, a silence descended.. Tony, with Big Mac and Mark alongside him, sat with the men and began to remind them where they had all come from. He touched on the difficulties they had all experienced in their personal lives and how the challenges had made them all the more stronger for it. Then he finally reminded them all of the value of their goal setting mentality they had adopted over the last year.

"Remember," he said "always take the objective or goal you want for your life to the very end of the line, to when you are old and grey. Yes, winning a few football games is awesome, but it should never be the overall objective as you need to always look at the bigger picture. Remember when I shared my goal, which is to leave this earth empty of every positive thought or encouragement I can bestow upon another. Once I have that mindset in place, I can just track back down the line to the here and now. I set myself daily goals and objectives and if I achieve them I will celebrate, but if I fail then it does not matter because my main objective is set in place for me, which allows me to just try again the next day."

"Yes today, gentleman, has been an amazing day and we should all revel in it; but as of tomorrow, we focus our sights again on the next game; whether it is league or cup it is irrelevant. Let's just play our football and enjoy it!" he pronounced.

" I'll finish with this," Tony continued. "Believing in something bigger or higher than you is the key".

And he finished there, before adding that Mark had arranged for them all to spend the evening at Giovanni's and to bring their wives or girlfriends, as tonight Handley Park Rangers would celebrate being in the semifinals of the FA cup!

43

The Semi Final – Almost there lads!

As access to just about any line of credit with every local transport company had either been abused beyond their standard terms or simply closed, Tony had no option but to be creative with the team's mode of transport for their semi final match. And this had been achieved by badgering John Vossa into submission to finally agree to pull in a few favours through his network of contacts within the motor industry. The lads, as agreed, had assembled early in the morning for a quick run followed by breakfast kindly laid on by Giovanni and his family. The lads, understandably, were a little jittery and some were beginning to allow their nerves to get the better of them; but that said they were in good spirits.

Breakfast consisted of espresso coffee, freshly squeezed orange juice followed by an Italian omelette with Giovanni's secret ingredients which, in fairness, turned out to be delicious. Giovanni asked if he could say a few words of encouragement to the team as they tucked into their food. He let them all know just how proud he was of them and how proud the late Brian

Hawkson would have been with this gifted group of men. Eventually, after Giovanni's rather long, drawn out speech, the squad headed down the High Street and back towards the club. A sense of tension continued to prevail amongst them as some of the players habitually over talked about nothing in particular, all with the express aim of calming their nerves. As the team came past the town's library, they noticed two stretch Hummer Limousines pulling into the club car park. They were soon laughing and jostling each other wondering who would be in the cars, especially the lead car as it was finished in bright pink. The lads were soon swarming around the cars, hoping to catch a glimpse of the famous occupants inside. Perhaps a celebrity well wisher had ventured out to see them off?

The mood soon changed in the camp when they realised that the cars were for them and before anyone knew it, the beginnings of a mutiny was assembling. Mark and Big Mac initially thought it was hilarious and were looking forward to seeing how Tony intended to talk his way out of it. But after watching Tony and John exchange some heated words, both Mark and Mac soon realised that somehow they would be roped in to cajoling the lads into the vehicles. Finally, everyone gathered round Tony, Mac and Mark. After a few gentle threats, silence descended and Tony spoke "Listen lads. Like you all, I'm slightly surprised myself with our mode of transport. Some of you may even be thinking what a laughing stock we are turning out to be, but let me just reaffirm to you all that we have earned our place in this semi final and that we are not here to make up the numbers. So, just to put your minds at rest; Mac, Mark and John along with all of your kit have kindly opted for, and I might add as their first choice, to ride in the front with Sheila's wheel whilst the rest of us will be riding in the more conservative Hummer." And with that, Tony spun on his heels, allowing pandemonium to break out behind him while Mac and Mark just looked at each other. John chased after Tony, like he was a referee, getting ready to protest but it was all in vain, as Tony had made up his mind, so within ten minutes both cars were loaded up and ready to leave.

Just before 10.00am, the cars pulled out of the car park with the pink lead car completely closed up, whilst the black Hummer, for at least the first 30 minutes of the journey, had all of the windows down and the sunroof fully retracted with music blaring, as many of the players waved to the people of the town who had turned out to see them off. Interestingly enough, not one of the players at that moment had an ounce of nervousness or fear in their minds; they were far too busy laughing or hiding from any traffic that surrounded them and this was to be intensified when the lead car experienced a flat tyre along the hard shoulder just past Scratchwood services. At the request of Tony, the entire squad had been tasked with either assisting with changing the wheel or carrying out some light exercise up and down the embankment. For any passing traffic, the scene must have looked bewildering but by then the team were starting to get in the zone as they prepared for the game ahead. In fact, the gauntlet laid down by Tony did no more than spur them on in their mission to continue their giant killing quest. Within the hour, the team were back on the road and on their way to the stadium. Once inside, they completed further training and warm up repetitions before stripping and readying themselves for the game ahead. Soon after, they took to the field of play for what would be an epic encounter that would last well past the 90 minute mark and into extra time.

The extra 30 minutes of play was not enough to separate the two teams from the dreaded lottery of sudden death penalties. The game had played out like a strategic game of chess. The Reds had chosen to mirror Handley Park with a 3-4-3 formation, which served as a huge compliment to the formidable tactics adopted by Handley Park throughout their rather unexpected but impressive cup run. You see, from the start, dominating possession had never really been Handley Park's objective, as they liked to play to their strengths, which were_ keeping it simple, playing a high line, intercepting and breaking up play to frustrate their opponents, biding their time and hitting their opponents hard on the counter whilst maintaining a strong, balanced shape at the back. And so with this in mind, The Reds completely disregarded their usual relentless attacking formation for a more strategic cat and mouse approach. From a tactical viewpoint, this made for a very impressive game plan but it did leave the fans a little wanting when it came to adrenalin filled, fast-paced, attacking football. With a little over 120 minutes of play now complete, it was up to the coaches to rally the troops and prepare their squads for penalties.

Tony gathered his team in a huddle. No one was allowed to sit, kneel or lay on the ground. They were all instructed to do no more than focus and listen to what was about to be said. Mark, as chaplain, was tasked with a simple prayer for the players, whilst Clay was earmarked by Tony as the man that would send the squad through to the cup final. Tony reminded Clay, in full view of the other players, about his amazing ability to see open play unfold before his very eyes in slow motion. This, of course, was difficult to explain, but Clay somehow possessed the skill and ability to watch situations happen and unfold in his mind in slow motion whilst being able to read and respond, not react impulsively but decisively and with a pace that was both clinical and rapid enough that it allowed him to intercept almost any shot on goal. Clay's ability was easily overlooked as it often happened so quickly, whilst at the same time looking almost clumsy as if he was acting on luck rather than sound judgement. In a nutshell, he made it look effortless and unassuming and that was why it had never been highlighted by the press or the media. But Tony knew that after this shoot out, win or lose, that henceforth, Clay Jackson would be in the national spotlight.

After the customary 10 minutes to organise the pecking order for spot kicks, both teams ventured out to the centre circle to wait their turn on this emotional rollercoaster. Clay received a quick neck rub from Big Mac. He looked Clay square in the eyes with the express aim of challenging his thought process. He wanted to convince him that he could do this and step up to the plate and be the 'man of the moment' but when their eyes met, instead of Big Mac reassuring Clay, Mac sensed it was the other way around. "I've got this Big Mac," was all Clay said, before spinning on his heels and heading over to the referee and opposing keeper. There was no need to worry tonight about the added advantage of fans behind the designated goal, as The Reds fans made up at least 95% of the people in the stadium. Clay listened intently to the referee as he explained what was expected from both goalies during the shoot-out. Normally the keepers would just go through the motions and nod their heads and focus more on composing their thoughts as they prepared for the job in hand, but not Clay. No, he wanted specifics. He wanted to fully understand where he was expected to stand and to what extent were his movements curtailed. The other team's goalie just looked on bemused, rolling his eyes in unison with the referee at, what to him, was inconsequential trivia. Tony noticed the reactions from both The Red's keeper and the referee as Clay questioned the rules and was encouraged as he'd sensed the ridicule. 'Good,' he thought to himself. "You just keep thinking that, "as my boy is about to kick-butt" he pronounced with satisfaction.

With all of the preliminaries now in place, it was the turn of Clay to face the number 1 penalty shooter for The Reds. Both Big Mac and Mark were unable to look as the ball was placed on the spot and the striker stepped back by three paces and composed himself in preparation to strike. There were no shenanigans, play acting or "Dudek dancing" from Clay. No, he just remained motionless as he stood on the goal line waiting for the shooter to make his move. There was no need for Clay to try and make himself look big in goal as he was already a man mountain, so instead he began the mental process of preparing his mind. Slowly he reduced his breathing and cleared his mind of every-thing except the man standing before him. He wasn't frantically trying to recall what historical preference the player had when it came to placing his shot, no, Clay was just in the moment, just breathing and allowing his mind to focus 100% on what was before him. He was in the zone. With the noise from the crowd now abated, it was just Clay and The Red's number 10 before him. Clay could hear his heart beating in his chest and as he focused on the player, he could sense the indifference within as the man wrestled with which option to take; would it be left or right, placing the ball far from the reach of this man mountain that stood before him or should he just thump the ball straight down the middle with all of his might? The agony within the striker was intense until finally, he threw caution to the wind and launched himself at the ball with the intention of placing it in the bottom left corner. The shot was good and left his design-er boot at full throttle, heading exactly where the striker had meant for it to go. The fans held their breath with many averting their gaze, whilst others were urging the ball on with their thoughts but for Clay, time stood still. He had no idea how, but he already knew that the ball would be heading towards him at probably 70 to 80mph, covering a distance of 36 feet which would likely take no more than just over half a second to reach its destination. He knew that the possibility of covering the 192 square feet of goal space was virtually impossible, and that if he planned to jump or dive, then it had to be in advance of the ball leaving the player's boot. But with all that said and done, he knew wholeheartedly that as soon as the ball left the spot that he would somehow be able to move in advance of the shot and prevent the ball from crossing the goal line. The save never looked heroic in any shape or form, more of a clumsy interception but it worked like a charm. As for number 10's impressive shot, it was intercepted by Clay's shin just as it was about to reach the goal line. The player was crushed by what he thought was a lucky save and headed back to his team mates at the centre circle with his tail between his legs.

Next up was The Red's goalie who swaggered past Clay heading to the goal line, but not before grabbing the ball and taking the opportunity to hand it to Sam, whilst attempting to stare him down, hoping to undermine his confidence. The attempt proved futile, as Mark had prepared him well for this moment. He'd introduced him to the ancient art of Poker by teaching him to not play the odds but instead play the man, and for this reason, Sam remained unperturbed as he proceeded to place the ball on the spot, whilst maintaining full eye contact with the goalie. He took a few steps back, slowed his breathing down a few notches before stepping up to pull the trigger. He'd already made up his mind where he would place the ball and had spent many hours on the training field fine-tuning his shooting skills. He'd paid no attention to the goalie, who'd attempted to put him off, instead he just visualised the ball breaking the side netting and putting Handley Park in the driving seat. Sam lowered his body and positioned his arms ready for launch time. One, two, three he was off and with no doubt in his mind, he hit that ball with all he could muster. The ball left the ground with full thrust, like a commercial airliner as it left the runway bound for foreign climates. It arched immediately away from the centre of the goal, heading towards the left post. The keeper guessed well and made an impressive dive off his goal line towards the ball but the distance he travelled just wasn't enough, as the ball seemed to curve round his fully stretched arms and beyond his reach straight into the left hand side netting. Sam raised both arms in triumph as he turned and raced towards his teammates.

The next two Reds penalties were wide of the goal however, Handley Park were unable to capitalise on their one nil cushion as the Red's goalie was starting to throw his weight about in front of goal by pulling off some rather theatrical saves which, of course, he felt compelled to gloat about, in-front of his adoring fans. The fourth Red's man to step up to take his penalty was their most expensive player on the pitch. He was from the Baltics and had arrived at the club some two years previous. He was a formidable midfield player and possessed that little bit extra that made him stand out from the crowd. He was strong and decisive in front of goal and would almost guarantee you twenty plus goals a season. He'd put a real shift in this afternoon and felt he deserved something from the game. He placed the ball on the spot, moving it around slightly until he was satisfied with its position and as he stood up he took a good look at Clay, who remained motionless in goal. He looked intently, not trying to unsettle him but more to get a better understanding of this man who stood before him and as the men exchanged glances the player realised instinctively that to underestimate Clay would be at his peril. There was something about this goalie that he just could not put his finger on and as he turned, measured his run up and prepared to take his penalty, he had a sudden notion; 'this keeper is far better than any of us realise' and as his skillful shot left his favourite left boot, he knew instinctively that Clay had it covered and sure enough there was that clumsy parry that moved the ball clear of the goal line. The two men shot a quick glance at each other again and The Red's player mouthed the word "effortless" towards Clay, which prompted him to just shrug his shoulders, as if to express no more than a fortunate run of play.

The Red's player turned and joined his teammates at the centre circle where he was met with the odd commiserative gesture, but he just shunned the response away and looking up, he said in a heavy accent to the team, "You won't get the ball past that goalie, he is better than you think."
The players just looked at each other with the impression that maybe their star man was just being a bit prima donnarish because he missed, but he looked at them all again and stated, "You will not get that ball past that man".
Now with four penalties taken and no goals achieved for The Red's team, it was up to Graham to step up to the plate. He was pretty nervous and would have happily avoided the task altogether but Tony had insisted on it informing him simply, "You can do this."
He made his way from the centre circle towards the penalty spot, where he fully expected to be met by the biggest ego on the pitch, who would, of course, go out of his way to unsettle him. But surprisingly, The Red's keeper had gone straight behind his goal line and waited patiently. This helped Graham's nerves to

settle and so he proceeded to mentally prepare and visualise where he would place his shot. Mark again had prepared his player well for this moment. He had reminded Graham of the time when Mark had climbed in his face and bawled him out about the next move he would make in his life, and sure enough, it had triggered a significant memory that would serve him well as he made his run up. Under his breath Graham declared; "I'm no longer a victim or a loser of this game I so love. I'm a winner. I will not bow down to what has gone before. I'm an overcomer." And with that he was off; thump, that ball was running at an alarming pace straight down the centre. If the goalie had been there, it would have been advisable for him to move out the way as it surely would have done some damage. As it turned out, the keeper opted to second guess and had launched himself to the right, well before the shot was taken and with that the game was over. Handley Park Rangers were in the "FA Cup final!"

The team stormed towards Graham, bundling him to the floor celebrating with joy but they all soon dispersed when they noticed Clay preparing to take a run and jump towards them all. After, they gathered around the dugout to celebrate with the rest of the team and their coaches. It was an unbelievable moment they would never forget, especially when Big Mac shouted for them all to look up; as the players looked to the crowd, they were met with the most amazing sound resonating around the ground. The entire stadium were chanting the name of Handley Park Rangers and it soon became apparent that all of the fans present wanted to celebrate with the team. Tony was completely overwhelmed by the response and commanded his players to get out there and enjoy the moment. As he turned towards Big Mac and Mark, he noticed them both sitting in the dugout, sobbing their hearts out with their heads in their hands. He went over to join them and sat patiently until they finished crying (boy, did those men have some tears in them). As they finally composed themselves, Big Mac looked to Tony and uttered "Thanks Tony. For too long I have carried so much pain and anguish and felt I would never be able to let go of what happened all those years ago. But finally, what with the number 96 emblem on our shirt sleeves and the amazing response from the crowd, I feel free" and with that the sobs broke out again.

Mark, with a voice overcome with emotion, choked back the tears and bawled, "I don't know how we pulled this off Tony? I'm not one easily surprised and like to think of myself as one step ahead of the game, but.... but...." and with that he began to blubber again.

Tony just shrugged his shoulders and shook his head to himself at the sight of these two battle wearied, hardcore characters that he'd grown to love so much and with that he turned and headed out onto the pitch to join his lads.

44

You're live on air with HP radio. Interview with Tony Jeffs, Billy "Big Mac" McGrath and Mark Dellany Smith.

Apparently cynicism gets easier with practice or so Charles was informed by an old school bud of his. You see Charles's mate, Ryan, now an acclaimed satirist, without doubt would best be described as your doyen of a cynic. For as far as he was concerned, Humpty Dumpty was pushed, he never fell and anyone who says otherwise is nothing but a wannabe conspiracy theorist looking for a cheap bite. All sounds highly irregular, I know, however, cynicism in its purest form is a destructive path for anyone to go down, including Ryan. Problem is what starts out as no more than an act of self preservation due to an embarrassing moment that required some form of atonement, eventually leads you down a path of passivity followed by a whole lot of nothingness, which in turn leaves you at the door of mediocrity until eventually, Charles's old mate Ryan can stand it no more and hits the proverbial autopilot switch in his head all with the express hope of instilling a little peace and semblance. Only thing is, now Ryan earns a living tearing a strip off people just for kicks and hopes that someday further down the line he can regain his humanity.

As for Charles, life at a tin pot local radio station is not enough and seeing his friend under the big lights enjoying the accolades whilst lining his pockets is more than he can bear. He needs his shot and decides he will not be left behind. Hence the desire to have Tony, Mac and Mark on the show as no one outgrows Charles Hayworth and right now these three coaches make the perfect meal ticket to get him out of here (or so he thought to himself)

Charles: HP show host: "I can't believe it listeners and I'm sure you can't too. But finally. At long last we have none other than two thirds of the coaching staff of Handley Park Rangers. Unfortunately "the running man" has been delayed but I'm told will be with us shortly and may even have one of the regular players with him once they've finished their run across the moors." Can I have a drum roll please ladies and gentlemen!!!

Big Mac: Not really his bag when it comes to interviews as he prefers to stay out of the limelight; "Thanks for having us on your show Charles!"

Charles: A little undecided as to how to proceed purely because he knows if he gets this interview right he will have at long last attracted the attention of some of the national shows. He thinks to himself; shall I go for glory or shall I play safe? And with so much at stake he takes the plunge and opts to go for glory. "Now. If I may, I'd like to start with you Tony. You must be feeling pretty good about yourself taking charge of such an ailing club and turning it around like you have? You surely must have some of the big boys knocking on your door trying to open up a dialogue?"

Tony: (Strike One. The coaches are not impressed!) After a brief pause for thought. He's disappointed because he now knows that Charles has taken the plunge and decided to feather his own nest at Handley Park's expense. Finally he responds somewhat tactically. "I'm not sure I understand your line of questioning Charles. Do you have a specific question as from where I'm sitting this club isn't about one particular person. No, it's about all of us as a unit including the good people of this town."

Charles: Under his breath; "likes to think of himself as a bit of a politician does he? We'll see! Let's see how he copes with this curved ball then." "Oh I get it Tony! So what you're saying is that all of this success must have been down to all of the hard work put in by Mike Phillips and Nigel Hawkson?" Again under his breath; "How d'you like them apples then guys?"

Tony & Big Mac: (Strike Two not looking good for Charles); "Tony, if I may, I'd like to step in here." Tony simply gesticulated with his hands gesturing for Mac to go for it. "Listen, Charles, I like you and your radio station and understand that you've had some fun and games along the way concerning the affairs of the club. Who wouldn't? So perhaps I need to make myself clear when I suggest to you that maybe you shouldn't waste this time as an opportunity for you to draw attention to yourself from some of the national radio stations." Charles pursed his lips for a second as he prepared to hit back with a cheap sarcastic side swipe. But not before Tony added; "It's not worth it son. I've seen him when he's angry and it's not pretty. So why don't you take five and think about asking us some more prudent questions and let's see if we can get this interview rolling!"

Charles; Feeling slightly out maneuvered begins to stammer somewhat before finally suggesting a short interlude and so prepares a song from his playlist. Now pretty mad, he opened his mouth as if about to say something; off air, but thought better of it. Thankfully his blushes were spared when Mark finally pitched up looking rather sweaty, closely followed by Clay as he ducked under the door frame at the same time blocking out most of the natural light in the room. Unfortunately Charles stay of execution was short lived as the song playing was about to finish and now he felt completely intimidated with the four men facing him. And what made matters worse was when Tony nodded that they were now ready to continue. Charles was completely thrown off course and looked unlikely to resume any time soon. It was Mark who finally bailed him out when he suggested that maybe he could ask about the clubs planned build up to the final. The song playing began to fade out which seemed to spark Charles back into life as he quickly mic'd up and began to speak; "And er welcome back folks to er HP Live on air where today we have not only the full management team of HPR but also their star attraction Clay Jackson!" And as Charles finished speaking he clearly heard the voice of Mac as he whispered "be careful son."

Charles; Could not believe he had been out played by these middle aged country bumpkins. Normally he could go toe to toe with the best of them and come out on top but not with these three no four men. At least, Charles thought to himself, I could have had some fun and games with Clay by twisting his words a little and taking him down a controversial path of spin but not with his baby sitters at hand. Finally Charles acquiesced his strategic plan of ridicule and rolled out a simple, more middle of the road line of questioning; "So guys! What's the plan as you lead up to the big day?"

Tony; "Ah thanks Charles." Tony lingered as he'd not quite finished with Charles yet as he sensed there was some kind of turmoil going on behind the scenes in his life. The silence was making Charles feel even more on edge but Tony was not fazed. Neither were Mac, Tony and Clay as they guessed he was up to something. Again Tony spoke; "Thanks Charles" but this time, with his head slanted, he looked even more intensely at Charles. Finally, now wagging his finger, he continued; "You know Charles, I sense that you're a really good presenter. In fact you're an absolute natural. I would even go as far as to say that your talents are wasted. Not because you are here, no. I like this place. No, it's to do with some kind of inner turmoil bubbling away in your mind. Would I be right in thinking that you possess this crazy ability to read people. You know, the ability to gauge what's going on in their world effortlessly. Question is though why do you choose to judge them rather than help them. You don't have to respond Charles because I can see it as clear as day on your face."

Charles looked dumbfounded let alone Mac, Mark and Clay who could not believe this conversation was going on live on air.

Unfortunately though Tony wasn't finished. "Oh come on Charles, don't get all riled up just because you're being challenged! Either way son, you know I'm right. What I want to know is what are you going to do about it? Are you going to keep chasing the tailcoats of your troubled pal in the hope of landing your alleged dream job at a national station or are you going to be honest with yourself and find your own lane. Your own purpose."

An awkward silence filled the place again. Charles, now completely bamboozled was lost for words and was not likely to recover anytime soon. In fact his only reaction was to rip his headset off and storm out the door. Mac, Mark and Clay turned to Tony as if to say something but it was Tony who spoke first; "Oh come on guys! You know I was right. I was just trying to help him."

Mac leaned in closer to Tony and spoke; "Yes I know Tony. But not live on air!" The penny at long last dropped for Tony as he'd realised the error of his ways and was about to go in search of Charles to apologise but it was Mark who stood from his stool and suggested that perhaps he could have a chat with him instead.

To cover the faux pas, the guys decided to commence a conversation amongst themselves about their plans for the build up week to the final. Whilst in the meantime the switchboard was buzzing off the hook with constant calls from listeners wanting to know more from Charles and Tony.

Clay; "D'you know I think it was a really great idea of Kieran's to have us all take the train together down to North West London and then head out to Brent Cross to buy some off the peg suits before converging on our budget hotel at Wembley Park. Forgetting the final for a minute I'm just so excited"

Mac; "Let's just hope they do a man mountain off the peg suit size at some of the stores."

Tony: "I have to say; Kieran and his team have been total lifesavers for the club. It's been an absolute pleasure having him around."

Mac; "Never thought I would say it but I can't argue there. I guess the cynic in me liked to always have the last word by surmising that there always has to be something in it for the interested party but for me Kieran is a true gent."

The conversation was beginning to wane that was until Mark returned with a far more composed Charles. Tony looked across at him as if to gesture some form of an apology but Charles just nodded in acknowledgement and busied himself with his mike as he prepared to re-engage with them. For a minute Tony was concerned that maybe Charles was about to commence a tit for tat retaliation but surprisingly he just eased his way back into the discussion and soon had full control of the men as he managed to pull some more interesting facts out of them including the team's desire to mingle with the fans as they headed down Wembley Way during the build up to the match.

Once the show was over Tony made his way across to Charles with the express aim of apologising to him profusely for his on air outburst. There really was no excuse but again surprisingly Charles just waved away his comments and suggested that maybe Tony was bang on the money regarding the civil war that had been raging within him for so many years. In fact, not only did he feel better but potentially he'd possibly found a better way to serve the good people of Handley Park by adjusting his radio show to incorporate a more engaging theme of people expressing how they felt. This was purely down to the fact that Tony had engaged so earnestly and maybe it should be Charles who needed to apologise.

Mac: "Go figure!" was all he said when the men left the radio station. "You're the only fella I know who could fall down in a field of horse manure and come out smelling of roses!" To which they all laughed. "Talking of horse manure. Who's for a coffee at Giovanni's?"

In unison Tony, Mark and Clay replied;"Only if you're buying" and with that the men made their way through the busy Market and across to their favourite cafe.

45

This is it boys!

For the first time in Tony's tenure as HPR coach, he sensed the presence of an old adversary; namely - doubt. Like a thief in the night, and without prior warning, it had come calling. It had also taken the trouble to invite a couple of its old pals, fear and worry, where together they pulled up a seat, right in the middle of the dressing room, ready to start a gigantic pity party. Tony knew that at some stage this was bound to happen, but today of all days? The timing sucked. He looked around at the men he had grown so accustomed to; they were no longer brothers in arms, they were family to him now. As far as Tony was concerned, win, lose or draw today, it did not matter as these lads and this experience was now etched on his heart forever. "But a win would be nice though," he said outright without realising it. The lads lifted their chins from off of their chest for a brief minute, looking up at Tony bemused. 'Bless them,' he thought 'they look like rabbits in the headlights.' Instinctively, he knew that any attempt of motivational slogans, speeches or cajoling was not going to cut the mustard. No, the team needed some divine intervention if they were to be stirred up for one last fight.

So, against all reasoning Tony sat down and closed his eyes and began focusing his mind, hoping for a miracle. Both Big Mac and Mark could also sense the air of indifference, coupled with a lack of self belief starting to creep in, but, like Tony, they chose to keep schtum hoping the men would shake off their nerves and focus in order to mentally prepare for the game ahead. Frank attempted to stir the lads a little by joking and bantering with a few of them hoping to catch a bite and fuel a wind up or two, but no one was in the mood.

Everybody was now kitted up and dressed ready but the heavy, solemn mood in the camp remained. That was, until at long last, a flicker of movement, as Clay Jackson stood up walked through the middle of them and took centre stage. Clay's presence was always impressive, at just a few inches under seven feet in height and with a body ripping in muscle at every orifice, but when it came to talking, well, he wasn't the best. But today, all of that was about to change as he began sharing, initially, about his life back home in The States and how his mum had raised him on her own, working a number of jobs. If it hadn't have been for his appearance, he would have been an easy target for the bullies at his local high school and not just for his awkward speech; his attire did not account for much either as money was so scarce. Clay freely admitted he was no academic, although he believed he had a gift of knowing when and when not to speak and right now was his time to speak. At that moment, Tony looked around and could see that everyone was captivated by what Clay had to say. And so he continued, as he shared a little about his days as a quarterback but not boastful in any way about some of the touchdowns he was credited for. No, he was more interested in talking about the togetherness of the team and the value it offered. From nowhere, he asked why all of them played football and what playing meant to them. But before anyone could consider or respond, he continued by sharing how in countries much poorer than theirs, footballers, who considered themselves a privileged few, believed that their mission was to rescue the self esteem of the workers who woke up early in the morning and returned home late at night. Clay stopped for a minute and looked at all of the men before continuing

"You know, we are a privileged few. We might not be millionaire household names with fast cars parked outside,well, maybe except for you John," to which they all laughed. "But all of you have fought long and hard and from what I can see without reward. Therefore, I say to you all right now; you've earnt this moment in time, let's not waste it. So my question to you is; are we ready? Are we ready? I say again, are we ready?"

In an instant, the atmosphere began to change, which all three coaches picked up on as they caught each other's eye with a knowing glance. Clay continued some more, "You know back home, just before a big game, me and the guys would perform a traditional chant to what we believed to be an old song from way back when, during the days of slavery. For me the song possessed a kind of hypnotic power that had the capability to wake any one of us from our reverie and help prepare us for whatever we were about to face. The chant we adopted was simple and rhythmic but would soon crank up as the team began to feel the beat and begin to let themselves go." He stopped for a moment to reflect before looking down at all of teammates who were now completely engrossed in his story. "Guys," continued Clay. "I know in my heart of hearts that we should adopt the same chant, but before we launch in, I thought it would be a good idea to replace one of the lyrics for what I believe is befitting of the occasion." Clay continued by asking another question, again not waiting for a response as he shared a story about the 33 Chilean miners back in 2010 that had been trapped in an old mine for 69 days, some

2,300ft below ground. The question he raised was; what was the message left written on the wall by the miners when they eventually left their entrapment? He paused briefly before continuing; the message was "God is with us." The reason for this inspiring story is purely because we have our own message etched on our wall back home which is "Deo Iuvante" - with God's help. The atmosphere in the room was becoming more intense now as he continued, "And I happen to believe that we could all do with a bit of His help right now. So who's up for the challenge?" whilst beating his chest menacingly with his fist. He continued beating his rather buff chest while leaning in towards each player as an act of defiance, challenging any fear they may still be feeling. It was as if Clay knew instinctively how to stir the mood in the room, because he now had everyone on their feet. Soon after, he began rocking his head and chanting in a deep hypnotic voice:

"We ready,

we ready,

we ready,

Deo Iuvante."

In an instant, some of the guys began dancing. One of the guys began adding some rhythmic melody as Clay waved his arm and said "Again" and this time a chorus of voices could be heard:

"We ready,

we ready,

we ready,

Deo Iuvante."

When they had gone round again he replied, "Again, come on louder!" and this time the guys began shaking the ceiling with their voices.

"We ready,

we ready,

we ready

Deo Iuvante."

Clay may have started on his own, but now they were all in full voice chanting and pointing and shouting until finally the whole place erupted including Tony, Big Mac and Mark who were busy clapping, jumping, hugging and screaming at the top of their voices. And the dancing, (or chucking shapes as they liked to call it) oh boy, that was just awful. Clay thought that some of those dudes needed some serious help. One of them looked like a drunk uncle at a wedding, whilst Darren and Frank attempted the moon walk with their studs on!

"In fact," declared John, "was it not Drax from the Guardians of the Galaxy, Vol 2 who stated 'There are two types of beings in the universe; those who dance, and those who do not or should not in our case." But at least it brought plenty of laughs. Finally after a good ten or fifteen minutes, they began to settle down and Tony stood before them and pronounced

"I do believe it is time now, gentlemen, to go and line up with our opponents in the tunnel. This will be game 735 of the FA Cup knockout tournament and we, Handley Park Rangers, are still standing. Now, who would like to join me one more time?" and with that all of the men, like a special forces army, stood in unison ready to file through the door, each one of them shaking hands with Tony, Mack and Mark as they passed by. They were ready!

As the three coaches went to join their players in the tunnel, it was Mac who spotted him first. Whether it was before the squad had seen him or not, he wasn't sure. Either way, it had no bearing as his presence now became clear to all personnel at the club. Inevitably it was Mac who spoke first. "How on earth did that man manage to wangle his way in here?"

A long silence ensued before Tony stepped forward and rather tactfully admitted that is was him who'd invited Nigel. Mac was lost for words and was unable to respond before finally blurting out "But why? All he's ever done for this club is try to bleed it dry! And if he wasn't doing that, he was busy stabbing us all in the back trying to sell the club off to the highest bidder!"

Tony turned to look, not just at Mac but Mark and the rest of the squad. He rubbed his cleanly shaven chin and slowly glided the back of his hand across his cheeks and again under his chin. "Listen guys! The main reason you're all here is because you all fought long and hard and went well above and beyond the call of duty. But there's also another reason, albeit relatively minor. And that one is down to none other than

Nigel Hawkson. You see, he's the one that has been that added ingredient throughout; that has driven us beyond ourselves! And the simple answer for that is that he never respected any of us. In fact, he never gave any of us a chance. He simply wrote us off and took what he thought was rightfully his. Now, if you are angry with him and are keen to avenge him in some way for what he's done, then I get it, I do. But for me, I see his actions as no more than that of an irritant. The proverbial parasite that has penetrated an Oyster and set off a process of layering as a form of defense until finally, you end up with a nacre, a mother-of-pearl. And in our case, I reckon it's a pretty big one! Now I'm not suggesting you stroll over and thank him for all he's done, but I feel the time is right for us to celebrate why we are here and prove not just to yourselves but to him as well what you guys are capable of! That's it for me guys. You probably won't believe me when I say it, but I'm thankful to him for sticking it to us."

It was Darren that cut in first, as he stepped out of the line-up and pointed towards Tony. "I think I realise now what both Mac and Mark meant when they described you as one crazy, danger-ous man." He laughed to himself before continuing "I'm ready, thanks to Clay, and I'm in! Who else is with this crazy guy?" And with that the chanting broke out again as they all declared that they were ready and willing and able to take the game to their opponents. In fact it took a number of FA officials to step in and calm the Handley Park squad down.

"Are there any other surprises you'd like to share before we continue?" declared Mark. "No that's it for now," laughed Tony, "just thought it would add to the fire before we stepped out."
"You're not far wrong there," suggested Mac.
"I know, sorry. No more surprises," added Tony.
"Now, back to the game if that's alright" said Mac."D'you think we can do it?"
Tony looked both Mac and Mark in the eyes before responding "One of my old heroes, the late Bobby Robson, in an interview after Italia 90 was asked to juxtapose how England would have fared in the final if they had made it past West Germany. His response was simple 'I'm not a betting man, but I would have put my house on England beating Argentina in the final.' And I, my friends, would do exactly the same right now, pitching our boys against any team."
And with that, the three of them stepped out through the tunnel toward the hallowed turf of Wembley stadium, ready to make some history.

THE END

9 780995 683730